"What was that?" he asked

"Fireworks," Destiny answered, glad he, too, had experienced the sensations.

Wesley broke from their embrace and left her alone with her stunned expression.

"I don't think so," he said.

The alarm in his voice filtered through her passion-laden brain. "What is it?"

She had barely gotten the question out when she heard the rapid succession of pops again. It took a second for the sound of glass shattering to register.

"Stay here!" Wesl— _____ ved to the door.

Destiny _____ le off the bed whe _____ arkened hallway. _____ lly functional, she began _____ hat was happening.

The unmistakable scent of gunpowder filled her nostrils as she followed the path Wesley had taken. She heard nothing above the pounding of her pulse.

Dear Reader,

Welcome to THE ROSE TATTOO! More than food and drink are served up in this friendly neighborhood bar/restaurant in historic Charleston, South Carolina. There's a double dose of danger and desire on the menu, as well.

Kelsey Roberts, whose first Intrigue back in 1993 made her a nominee for Best New Writer, brings her deft touch for mystery and romance to this suspenseful trilogy.

At The Rose Tattoo, you will meet proprietor Rose Porter and all the staff and patrons who somehow find danger...*and* the romance of a lifetime!

If you missed the last two books— *Unspoken Confessions* and *Unlawfully Wedded*, check the back pages for a chance to order them. You, too, can become a regular at The Rose Tattoo!

Sincerely,

Debra Matteucci
Senior Editor and Editorial Coodinator
Harlequin
300 E. 42nd St.
New York, NY 10017

Undying Laughter
Kelsey Roberts

Harlequin Books

TORONTO • NEW YORK • LONDON
AMSTERDAM • PARIS • SYDNEY • HAMBURG
STOCKHOLM • ATHENS • TOKYO • MILAN
MADRID • WARSAW • BUDAPEST • AUCKLAND

For the one person who has kept me sane for almost
fifteen years—Bob, I love you with all my heart.

I would gratefully like to acknowledge the assistance of
Pat Harding, Kay Manning and Carol Keane of Charleston,
South Carolina: my crack research team.

ISBN 0-373-22334-X

UNDYING LAUGHTER

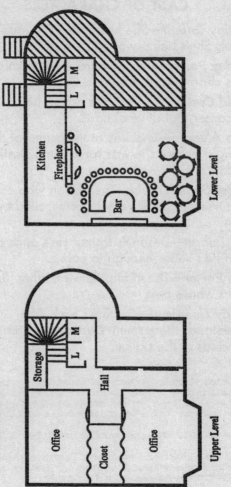

THE ROSE TATTOO

Upper Level

Office

Closet

Office

Hall

Storage

L | M

Lower Level

Kitchen

Fireplace

Bar

L | M

CAST OF CHARACTERS

Destiny Talbott—She has nothing to laugh about. She's being wooed by a stalker.

Wesley Porter—The chivalrous white knight. He is charming, if a bit peculiar.

David Crane—As Destiny's agent, he controls her career, but at what cost?

Gina Alverez—She was at the center of the limelight before she was forced into Destiny's shadow.

Walter Sommerfield—The patron who controls the purse strings. He's being controlled by a ghost.

Carl Talbott—Destiny's father. He's annoying, when he's sober enough to care.

Rose Porter—The manipulative mother. She knows what's best.

Shelby Hunnicutt—Destiny's rock. She understands the torment Destiny is suffering at the hands of the stalker.

Prologue

"He's out there!"

Destiny Talbott's violet eyes fixed on her friend's concerned reflection in the mirror. Gina's slender form seemed to heave under the weight of her urgent, shallow breathing.

A placating sigh escaped over full, rosy lips. "For God's sake, Gina, don't start *that!*" Destiny was mildly annoyed as she watched Gina anxiously twist her long-fingered hands into a knot of deep brown skin. Spinning, Destiny turned the chair in order to face the taller woman.

"That man gives me the creeps," Gina persisted. "There's something evil in the way he just sits there, staring at you. You're blinded by the lights, but I've watched him while you're up on stage. I tell you, he's freaky!"

Standing, Destiny tugged off the protective cloth she wore when applying stage makeup and tossed it onto the dressing table. Bottles clinked and swayed but none toppled. "Your imagination is getting the better of you," she said with more conviction than she actually felt. Ignoring Gina's grunt of disagreement, Destiny bent forward at the waist, then began to fe-

verishly brush volume into her mane of silky blond
hair.

"Five minutes, Ms. Talbott!" a male voice shouted
from the other side of the door.

"You got it!" she yelled back.

Gina reached out and placed a tentative hand on
Destiny's forearm. "Think, girl." The tone of the
voice was almost pleading, and at strict odds with the
harsh Brooklyn accent. "I'm sure he's the one who's
been sending you the flowers and . . . the notes."

A shiver danced along her spine, but Destiny managed to keep her expression bland. "I think you're
overreacting. And anyway, he doesn't look like the
type." Of that she was only mildly confident.

When Gina had first noticed the man, Destiny had
made a point of checking him out. While she secretly
admitted he looked out of place in the rowdy, younger
crowd she tended to attract, he didn't impress her as
being threatening. And the notes were nothing if not
threatening.

"We're ready, Ms. Talbott!"

Sucking in one deep breath, Destiny took one final
glance in the brightly lighted mirror. Giving Gina's
hand a light squeeze, she moved toward the door.

The muffled sound of the crowd caused a familiar
and immediate reaction. Adrenaline rushed through
her small frame, and her heart pounded against her
ribs.

"Ladies and gentlemen, the Miami Comedy Club
is proud to present Destiny Talbott!"

The roar as she stepped onto the stage was nearly
deafening in its intensity. The wooden floor beneath
her feet vibrated in sync with the applause. Clasping
the microphone in one professionally manicured hand,

Destiny gave a warm smile that produced yet another outburst of hearty appreciation.

"Hi, folks," she began as she walked back and forth on the planked floor, speaking into the bright void created by the harsh spotlights. "I always start by explaining my name. Only two hippies would dare name their child something as ridiculous as Destiny. My folks were definitely confused back then. My father was a Jehovah's Witness and my mother was an atheist. So..." She paused. "I spent my childhood knocking on doors for no reason. I'm originally from D.C—" A smattering of applause indicated there were a few residents of the nation's capital in her audience. "Washington is the home of our judicial system. In fact, we Americans are so hung up on compassionate justice that before we execute someone by lethal injection, we swab their arm with alcohol." Destiny waited for the rumble of laughter to die down before continuing. "I'm getting my mail forwarded here, and what do you know but I got an invitation telling me my high school reunion is scheduled for this spring. This basically means that four hundred or so people have about six months to lose fifty pounds and make something of themselves." Smiling, Destiny pulled the microphone fractionally closer to her glossed lips. Wrapping herself in the ensuing laughter, she continued her routine....

HE WATCHED HER, pure hatred glistening in his eyes. Lifting his glass to his mouth, he listened as the audience responded to her. They were fools, all of them. Couldn't they see what she really was? A user... and a whore. He saw through all her polish and glitter. When she smiled it made him want to stand and scream. Instead, he took a long swallow of his Scotch, enjoying the painful warmth as it slid down his constricted throat. He would be patient. Everything was planned.

As his eyes followed her movements across the stage, he played it all out in his mind. She'd beg, he knew that. Clearly he envisioned her huge eyes wide open and filled with the fearful certainty of her impending death. He'd make sure she suffered first.

Another response from the audience jarred him back to the present. Fixing his eyes on her, he was careful not to reveal any emotion. The sheer hose encasing her legs shimmered in the lights. He would wait until the time was right.

"YOU'VE BEEN GREAT! Thanks!" Destiny bounced off the stage as the audience chanted her name.

"You were hot tonight!" David Crane, her manager, said as he handed her a towel.

"Thanks!" she said and took the glass of water thrust in her direction. "This was my best show yet!"

"You say that every night," David countered as his hand went to the small of her back, leading her in the direction of her dressing room.

"Tonight was... I don't know, I just felt a certain electricity from the audience. It was a rush!"

Pushing open the door for her, David nudged her inside the small dressing room. The scent she had grown to detest brought on a sudden paralysis. It was the heavy, sweet aroma of gardenias. A chill, fierce and overpowering, settled on her like a heavy blanket.

"Blast it!" David bellowed.

She stood frozen just inside the door. David pushed past her and went over to the offensive pot of blossoms. Slowly he pulled the small white rectangle from among the flowers and tore into the envelope.

Chapter One

The flight from Miami to Charleston went smoothly, except for Destiny's lingering anxiety over the gifts she'd received the previous evening.

"Hopefully, he'll stay in Miami," she said to Gina as they sat in the back seat of a cab.

Gina frowned. "Don't bet on it. He's managed to make all your club dates for the past six months."

A shiver racked her small frame, but she said nothing. Gina, her personal assistant, had already suggested that she cancel this last engagement just to be on the safe side.

"Maybe he's tired of hearing the same material over and over," she said, forcing some lightness into her tone. "Maybe that detective David hired will figure out who he is."

Destiny felt the corners of her mouth turn down. The detective had missed their last meeting, so she had little faith that the rumpled detective had come up with anything substantial.

"Forget my fervent fan," Destiny told her friend. "Let's focus on something more upbeat, like the possibility of the network picking up my pilot."

Gina sighed and leaned her head against the back of the seat. "I could get used to L.A.," she said wistfully. Her hand automatically moved to her right leg, rubbing the carefully hidden scar Destiny knew ran the full length of her thigh. "The weather out there will do my leg some good. Might even take up roller blading."

Destiny laughed. "I think your doctor would nix that idea."

She watched as Gina's expression grew sad. "From graceful model to limping lump, all in one night."

Destiny said nothing. There was nothing to say. Nothing she hadn't said time and time again during the four years since the accident.

"That's Fort Sumpter," the driver announced as they wove their way over the uneven streets of Charleston.

"Maybe we'll take a day and sightsee," Destiny suggested.

"You never sightsee," Gina countered. "You're always too busy working on perfecting your routine."

"Am not."

"Are too."

"Wrong."

"Right," Gina huffed. "And I like David."

Rolling her eyes, Destiny wasn't in the right frame of mind to rehash the long-standing rivalry between the duo. David and Gina were her friends as well as her employees. Besides which, Gina, she had learned, didn't like too many people. She was Destiny's exact opposite. And a definite thorn in David's side. Sometimes she had the distinct impression that Gina went out of her way to make David's job harder. This trip was a perfect example. David had arranged for them to stay in one of the swankiest hotels in downtown Charleston. Gina had made arrangements for them to rent two of the villa units at the beach outside the city. Of course, it left Destiny in the uncomfortable position of choosing between the two. It was a no-win situation, and she was currently on David's list because she'd chosen the beach over the city.

"Wait!" she called out suddenly.

The cabby brought the car to a screeching halt.

"What?" the driver and Gina said in unison.

"There's The Rose Tattoo," she said, pointing to the historic building with the wooden sign in front. "Let's stop in."

"What about our luggage?" the ever-practical Gina noted.

"You go on to the beach, then come back," Destiny instructed as she opened her door. "Take as long as you need. I'd love to get a feel for the place."

"You can do that tomorrow." Gina was still grumbling when Destiny closed the door and walked across the black-and-white-checkered tiles leading up to the front door.

Her hand closed on the brass handle and she gave a tug. Nothing. She tugged again as her eyes found the hours listed on a rectangular sign in the window.

"Great," she grumbled, checking her watch, then squinting against the early-morning sunlight. Destiny was about to turn back toward the street in search of a cab when a deep, sexy voice stopped her dead.

"It's you," he said as he pulled open the door.

She had to concentrate hard to keep her mouth from dropping open in an appreciative response to this gorgeous man. "Must be sunstroke," she said under her breath before flashing him her brightest smile.

His stomach knotted as if an elephant had kicked him—*hard*. She was even more beautiful than the photograph hanging above the bar. On more than one occasion, he had cynically remarked that the picture had to have been retouched. It wasn't possible for any living creature to be that beautiful, that perfect. He was wrong.

"Destiny Talbott," she said as she offered him her dainty hand.

Her skin was warm and soft, a perfect complement to the deep tan that naturally heightened the unusual shade of her eyes. And the way the sun shimmered off those long tresses of pale blond hair—he swallowed as he reluctantly dropped her hand.

"Do you have a name?" she asked, a teasing look in her eyes.

The fraction of a second it took him to recall his own name seemed to amuse her all the more.

"Wesley Porter," he mumbled, feeling his cheeks warm slightly as he ushered her inside the empty restaurant.

His palms were actually moist by the time they reached the bar, where his books were stacked high next to a mug of long-forgotten coffee.

"We weren't expecting you until this afternoon," he said.

Sliding onto one of the bar stools, Wesley battled to keep his eyes off the incredibly shapely legs peeking out from beneath her skirt.

"Spur-of-the-moment," she explained. "When I saw the place, I just couldn't resist taking a sneak peek."

He felt one of his brows arch high on his forehead. "Do you always act on your impulses?"

She smiled again. "Is that a question? Or a *really* bad come-on line?"

"Sorry," he mumbled, studying the backs of his hands. "I guess it's all this scholarly pursuit. I tend to ask questions a lot."

"A bar-owning student?" Destiny asked after glancing at his textbooks.

"My mother owns the place. I'm just helping out while I study for my boards."

"Rose," she said, nodding. "David's mentioned her."

"David?"

"My manager," she said as she boldly slid off the stool, went behind the bar and poured herself a cup of coffee.

Wes wasn't sure what bothered him more, the fact that she seemed so at home in a strange environment, or that he'd been so enthralled with her legs that he hadn't even thought to offer her the most basic of hospitalities.

"This is great," she said, hugging the mug in both hands. "I should have been entitled to a refund from the airlines for that stuff they foisted off on Gina and me this morning."

"Gina?"

"My personal assistant," she said as she came back and took the seat next to his. He smelled the faint scent of her perfume, and the words "utterly feminine" floated through his thoughts as he watched her felinelike movements. No wonder she was a popular performer, he thought. As far as he was concerned, she didn't have to tell the first joke. He'd probably pay good money just to watch her walk down the street.

"So," she began with a wicked light in her violet eyes, "do you just ask questions, or do you occasionally talk all on your own?"

"Depends," he returned, feeling the corners of his mouth respond to her ever-present smile. "I guess I've had my nose in these books for so long that I'm sort of out of practice."

"You?" she scoffed.

His head fell slightly to one side and he regarded her for a protracted second. "Meaning?"

"Back up," Destiny answered. "What exactly are you studying for?"

"Psychiatric boards."

"You're a shrink?"

"In training."

"Lord," she mumbled just before bringing the mug to her bow-shaped lips.

"I'll take that to mean you aren't fond of my profession?"

Her initial response was a small shrug of her shoulders. "Not my call," she told him. "I just think there's something perverse about delving into people's private lives."

He smiled at her. "This from a woman whose private life manages to grace the tabloids on occasion?"

"Point," she conceded. "You read the tabloids?"

"Only when I'm standing in the checkout line at the store."

"That's what everybody says. Except that those rags have higher circulation numbers than the *New York Times*."

A shrink, she thought to herself. Too bad. The first nice-looking doctor she ever meets turns out to be a psychiatrist. Heaven knew the very last thing she needed in her life was analysis.

Whoa! her brain screamed. This man wasn't exactly "in her life."

"Can I see the rest of the place?" she asked, wondering why she felt such an overwhelming sense of regret. It hardly made sense. She would be in Charleston all of six weeks. Then, hopefully, she'd be off to Los Angeles *and* her own television show.

"Sure thing," Wesley answered, reaching into the front pocket of his jeans and producing a ring full of keys. "Follow me."

Hopping off her stool and depositing her empty mug on the polished bar, Destiny silently admired the physique of the man ahead of her. His shoulders were broad beneath the preppy polo shirt. His waist and hips were trim, though he didn't impress her as the type to spend hours working out. He did, however, impress her as one heck of a sexy man.

With the exception of David, her world was filled with overweight, cigar-chewing club owners. This dark-haired intellectual man, with bedroom blue eyes hidden behind tortoiseshell glasses, was refreshing. He had jump-started her hormones in ways she had long ago suppressed.

Wesley led her through an immaculately clean kitchen and out the back door. The aroma of wisteria competed with the less-than-pleasant odors coming from the Dumpster.

"It's very deceptive from the street," she said, quickening her step to keep pace with his long strides.

"Charleston Single Houses were built on these long, narrow lots in order to capture the breeze coming off the water. Think of it as eighteenth-century air-conditioning.''

"Good line." She laughed. "Can I steal it for my routine?''

"Absolutely.''

Following him along the stone path, Destiny was immediately impressed by the condition of the long, rectangular sign hanging over the double doors. She was also vainly impressed by the large photograph of herself plastered above the door. After all this time, the words Appearing Nightly still gave Destiny a thrill.

The thrill faded quickly when she caught sight of the large box near the front door.

"Not again," she groaned.

"Not again what?'' Wesley asked her, genuine concern in his deep voice.

"I hope you have a girlfriend, Dr. Porter," she said, trying to keep her tone light.

"Why?''

"Because," she began as they reached the package covered by bright green floral wrap, "she'll think you're wonderful. But if I were you, I'd lose the card first.''

Wesley had begun to reach inside the paper when Destiny automatically grabbed for his hand. His skin was heated beneath her palm, momentarily distracting her.

"Don't bother," she said.

But apparently *this* man had a mind of his own. Destiny's hand fell away as he gently removed the envelope and pulled the card from inside.

His brows drew together as he read what she knew was the neatly typed message: SOME DIE LAUGHING.

Chapter Two

"What the hell does this mean?" Wesley demanded, waving the small card in his hand.

"It means I have an admirer with an even sicker sense of humor than my own," she answered, trying to make light of the situation. "If I ever find out who has been sending these to me, I'll refer them to you for professional help."

It was obvious from the ominous expression in his blue eyes that Dr. Porter shared Gina's concern over the succession of notes.

"How long has this been going on?"

Averting her eyes from the potted blossoms, Destiny answered, "About three months."

"Have you contacted the authorities?"

She met his gaze. "Do you have any idea how many cities I've been in during that time?"

Wesley shook his head.

"My manager did hire a private detective," she began, unable to keep the disgust out of her voice. "He proved himself completely inept, to the point of not even bothering to show up last night. Instead, I received a crumpled bill from his office, along with a poorly typed memo indicating that Greg Miller, private investigator, hadn't uncovered squat."

"Then maybe you should hire someone here."

"And waste more money?" she scoffed. "No, thanks. I'm sure whoever is sending these things will eventually get the hint. Or," she added as she leaned closer, "the florists will run out of gardenias, and he'll be out of luck."

"This note doesn't give me the impression that we're dealing with an admirer," Wesley told her. "It's too threatening. Too indicative that he is not overly fond of you."

Destiny rolled her eyes. *"Fond?"* she repeated with a throaty laugh. "Live dangerously, Dr. Porter. This bozo obviously hates me. But that's okay, I hate gardenias. So I guess he and I are running about even."

She watched as deep lines appeared at the corners of his eyes and mouth.

"Lighten up, Doctor. I'm not saying I'm thrilled by his persistence, but he's hardly overtly threatening. He hasn't come near me."

"Why are you so convinced it's a man?"

"Gina's picked him out of the audience. Wait until tomorrow night. If he comes, which he always does, I'll have Gina point him out to you."

"Did your assistant have a vision, or is there something in particular about this man that makes you believe he's your morbid admirer?"

"Can we get out of the sun?" she asked, not really interested in discussing the matter any further. Lord knew, it was a topic both Gina and David had beaten into the ground during the past several months.

"Sorry," she heard him mumble as he slipped a key into the ornate lock and opened the door.

It took several seconds for her eyes to adjust to the shadowy interior, even after he'd flipped a switch to turn on dim, period chandeliers.

"Wow," she said as she admired the long, rectangular room. Tables were arranged with wide aisles leading up to a small, but certainly sufficient, stage. The lighting she saw at the base of the stage was fine upon inspection. All in all, The Rose Tattoo promised to be a fairly decent engagement. "When David told me I'd be playing in an outbuilding, I sure wasn't expecting anything like this."

"That's because my oldest boy and his wife did the renovations."

Destiny twirled around at the sound of the female voice echoing through the room. A woman she placed somewhere in her early fifties sashayed toward them. Her outfit was outrageous—animal-print, skintight pants, a form-fitting blouse and bleached hair that nearly touched the ceiling. Garish clothing aside, Destiny was drawn to the woman's warm, welcoming smile.

"I'm Rose Porter," she said, extending her hand.

"Nice to meet you."

She turned to Wesley and said, "I saw the flowers outside. Your idea?"

Wesley shook his head. "I'm afraid they came with Miss Talbott," he answered dryly.

"Maybe we should make it a practice to send all our performers a little something," Rose said thoughtfully. "Maybe an Elvis tape."

Destiny watched as Wesley tried to hide a cringe behind square-tipped fingers. "We'll think about it."

"Anything you need," Rose began, "just let us know."

"I'm sure everything will be fine," Destiny answered. *Especially if I get to catch the occasional glimpse of Dr. Porter while I'm here.*

"I'VE CALLED THE STATION house," Gina was saying, her words running together in an agitated string.

Destiny had barely time to deposit her purse on the rattan sofa before her friend had launched into a long, involved explanation for her failure to show up at The Rose Tattoo. Destiny had stayed through dinner, at Rose's insistence. Unfortunately, Dr. Porter had disappeared before the lunch crush.

"I can call Western Union and make an immediate cash transfer. I think they said five hundred dollars for the bond."

"Don't bother," Destiny said with a sad sigh.

Gina's faced wrinkled in astonishment. "What do you mean?"

"He can spend the night in jail. God knows he's done it often enough before."

She walked over to the refrigerator and rummaged around until she found a diet soda, then lifted one of the leaded glasses from a neatly arranged tray. Each ice cube made a pleasant sound as she dropped it into the glass. She retrieved the bottle of soda and poured herself a generous portion.

Gina stood a few feet away, her hands resting on her nonexistent hips. Destiny never ceased to be amazed by the slenderness of the woman. She often remarked that even during the throes of PMS, Gina never managed to balloon above a size three. The fact that she was five-eight in her stocking feet mattered little, or that she still carried herself like the famous cover model she had once been.

"C'mon Destiny, Carl's your father. And your mother was really adamant when she called."

"I'll bet she was." Destiny smiled, easily imagining her mother's response to her former husband's latest predicament. In spite of the divorce that had taken place more than twenty years earlier, Chief Judge Mona Talbott still monitored the activities of her parasitic ex-husband. "My mother will survive." Destiny took a long swallow of her soda, allowing it to slide smoothly down her throat while pushing the memories of Dr. Porter to the back of her mind. Silently she told herself that her reaction to the man was simply the result of too many months on the road and not enough dates. Still, she just couldn't seem to rid the image of his dark hair and light eyes from her brain.

Gina's pretty face was a collage of concern and frustration as she watched Destiny refill the glass. "More flowers?"

"Uh-huh," Destiny grumbled into the glass.

"That's it!" Gina bellowed, raising her arms and allowing them to slap loudly against her thighs. Destiny found herself sneaking a peek at the lower portion of the ragged scar marring the brown-skinned woman's otherwise perfect leg.

"Girl, you'd better call someone. How about the police?"

Massaging the tension in her neck, Destiny offered a wan smile. "And tell them what? I'm Destiny Talbott and I'd like to report a delivery of flowers. I don't want my name and face plastered on the cover of every grocery-store rag. Not now. Not when I'm this close." She pinched her thumb and forefinger in front of her eyes, barely allowing light to pass between the small opening they formed. "I'd be labeled a paranoid crazy."

"Get serious, Destiny. You can't just ignore all the threats and stuff. Your buddy David isn't capable of handling this situation. It's gotten way out of hand, and you can't keep pretending that it isn't happening."

"I'm giving it my best shot."

"Fine. Do what you want. You will, anyway." Gina pointed a long, tapered finger at Destiny, shaking it for emphasis every now and then. "I don't mean to criticize your original patron saint, but David seems to worship the paycheck he gets from Sommerfield, not to mention—"

"Leave it alone, Gina."

Destiny's body tensed. *What if? No!* her brain screamed. It couldn't be David. It had to be a crazy person, and she wasn't about to let some lunatic exploit her—not now.

"Fine," her friend responded, clearly hurt. "And what about your father?"

"We'll wire the money in the morning. A night in jail will be good for him."

"What am I supposed to tell your mother? She's depending on you to take care of this."

"And I will. Only it will be tomorrow instead of the moment her majesty issues the order."

Destiny brushed past Gina, no longer interested in the conversation. Her whole body ached with the need to relax.

The second story of the villa sported an impressive master suite. The room must have been twenty-five by twenty-five, with adjoining dressing areas and a bathroom large enough to accommodate a family of six with room to spare.

Kicking off her shoes, Destiny pulled her dress over her head as she walked to the bath. The marble floor was refreshingly cool against her feet. The room smelled of exotic tropical fruits. She considered taking a long, hot bath, but opted instead for a long soak in the hot tub out on the patio. Letting pulsating streams of hot water rush over her body was a sure-fire way to wash away any lingering traces of her anxiety.

Removing the rest of her clothes, Destiny discarded them carelessly in a pile. As she stood completely naked, she ignored the pang of guilt trying to weave its way into her consciousness. Leaving her father in jail wasn't as easy a decision as she'd let on. In spite of everything, he was her father and she loved him.

Taking a few hairpins off the vanity, she secured the knot at the nape of her neck and willed herself not to think about her father's all-too-familiar plight.

"Blast you, Carl!" she whispered to her reflection.

Grabbing the soft white terry robe from a hook on the back of the bathroom door, Destiny sat on the edge of the bed to wait until she no longer heard Gina moving about in the rooms below. She was tired, too tired for another well-intended confrontational scene with her friend.

It wasn't long before she padded down the stairs, through the streaks of shadows and light from the moon sneaking in between the blinds. Carefully she opened the French doors that led to the tiled patio. "So far, so good," she whispered, her voice drowned out by the gentle rustling of the wind through the oleander bushes and the distant crash of waves from the Atlantic.

Dropping the robe, Destiny stepped down into the circular tub. Heat from the water rose in a swirl of steam before floating off on the breeze. The powerful jets forced ribbons of bubbles over her body, kneading her tense muscles like a patient lover. Closing her eyes, Destiny sank lower, allowing the swirling streams of water to work their magic. It was like being drugged, lulled into a sense of blissful relaxation.

"Miss Talbott?"

Her eyes flew open to find two figures near the back gate silhouetted in the moonlight. They were both tall and broad shouldered—and one was recognizable. Her eyes seemed determined to fix on that one form. The sinewy way his body tapered from those shoulders into that very sexy lean waist, she was absolutely certain she was looking at the outline of Wesley Porter. But then she recalled the voice saying her name. It was a voice she didn't recognize.

Instantly thinking of the flowers and the notes, Destiny screamed for Gina. The sound of her voice echoed in her own ears as she groped at the edge of the hot tub for her robe. Neither man moved in that fraction of a second.

Bright lights flooded the patio, blinding Destiny as she pulled the robe into the water. The sodden garment was immediately heavy and difficult to maneuver through the water.

"Up!" Gina's commanding voice split the night. "Get your hands up where I can see them! Now!"

Destiny backed out of the tub, wrapping the robe around her as she went.

"You okay?" Gina asked, her brown eyes never wavering from the pair standing awkwardly under the lights, their hands high in the air.

"I'm fine," Destiny answered in a high-pitched voice. Gina, wearing nothing but a flimsy teddy, stood with her legs shoulder width apart, her small silver revolver pointed in the direction of the intruders.

"Go in and call the police," Gina said. "I'll keep them here."

"Maybe not," Destiny said as she shook the fog of fear from her thoughts. "Sorry, Officer Gina. That's Dr. Porter from The Rose Tattoo."

"Oops," Gina said in a small voice as she lowered the gun.

Dylan fished inside his jacket pocket and retrieved his identification. He held it out for them between his thumb and finger in a very nonthreatening manner.

It seemed appropriate that Destiny be the one to examine his ID while Gina allowed the gun to dangle at her side. With a wad of wet terry cloth in her fist, she moved forward, barely aware that the full length of her leg was revealed with each step.

Standing in the shadow of the uncharacteristically silent Wes, Destiny scanned the laminated photo and found out that Dylan was some sort of agent for Alcohol, Tobacco and Firearms.

"Get your permit, Gina," she said. "Agent Tanner probably isn't too keen on having a gun waved in his direction."

"Okay," Gina said just before scurrying off.

Then Destiny got mad.

"Just what in the hell do you think you're doing on *my* patio in the middle of the night!" she bellowed at Wes, certain this late-night call was all his idea. She looked up into his blue eyes. The flash of amusement she saw there only added fuel to the fire of her anger. "And why did you drag him along?"

Grinning down at her from his superior height, Wesley said, "I called Dylan and asked him to help out. He's taking time away from his wife and new daughter just for you."

"Thank you," she mumbled. "But couldn't all this have waited until morning?"

Wesley crossed his arms in front of his chest, grinning like the proverbial cat, and said, "Probably. But then I would have been deprived of the opportunity to see you naked."

Chapter Three

"See me naked?" Destiny repeated blankly, lowering her eyes to her partially covered body. "You pig," she grumbled, adjusting the waterlogged robe to completely cover herself. "At best you got a cheap peek."

"Really?" Wesley asked in a bland voice. Then he leaned closer and spoke into her ear. "There isn't anything cheap about that cute little birthmark you have to the left of your navel. It's about an inch or two below your brea—"

"That's enough," she interjected, shoving him before he could finish humiliating her.

Cursing, Wesley hit the water with a loud splash and an even louder expletive.

"Watch your language, Doctor," she purred before making a mad dash toward the house.

"Don't let Porter drip on the hardwood," she instructed the stunned-looking Gina as she raced up the stairs. "Offer them a drink or something while I get dressed, please."

"Whatever you say."

Destiny had a limited selection in her closet. It wasn't that she couldn't afford a decent-size wardrobe, it was simply a matter of practicality. Living for a week here, a month there wasn't exactly conducive to becoming a clotheshorse.

"Please let them sell that pilot," she prayed as she towel dried her body and pulled on a sweat suit in a muted shade of mauve. Glancing at her reflection, she knew she didn't have time to do anything with her unruly mass of hair, so she simply left the pins in place and shoved any stray strands behind her ears.

She felt her cheeks warm as she remembered the deep, husky whisper of his voice when he'd commented on her birthmark. The memory alone was enough to make her body come to life with a series of electric pulsations that radiated from the core of her being outward to her fingertips.

"You're being stupid," she told herself as she hopped on one foot and forced the other into one tight espadrille. Wesley was definitely not her type. He was obviously a mamma's boy. Why else would he still be hanging around The Rose Tattoo with his mother? And she wasn't about to take on another needful man in her life.

She switched positions as she pulled on the other shoe. "For heaven's sake!" she scolded herself. "Stop acting like the guy just proposed. You've known him all of fourteen hours. He's hardly *in* your life."

Destiny found Dylan and Wes seated on the comfortable living room furniture. Actually, Wesley was on a pile of beach towels, his black hair slicked off his forehead. Dylan was nursing a beer, while, she noted, the wet one had opted for a soft drink. *Easy, girl,* her conscious warned.

"Sorry we disturbed you," Dylan said to her, though he was glaring at his companion. "But Wes led me to believe that this was something of an emergency.''

"Emergency?'' she echoed.

Wes's eyes darkened to an almost blackish blue as he gave her a reproachful look. "I saw your expression this afternoon when you got those flowers. It doesn't exactly take a member of Mensa to see that you have a possible stalker on your hands.''

"*Has* someone been stalking you?'' Dylan asked.

Destiny went to the bar and poured herself a glass of diet soda, wondering where Gina had disappeared to. "I have gotten a few strange notes and some flowers.'' Offering them her best stage smile, she added, "Most girls dream of getting flowers on a regular basis.''

"You aren't most girls,'' Wesley said softly.

Destiny felt her face redden with warmth as his eyes lingered on her mouth.

"You look very nice when you aren't all painted up,'' he commented.

She let out a small laugh. "Obviously, you've never worked under the glare of footlights, Doctor,'' she told him. "Without all that paint and glitter, I wash out like a ghost.''

Wes looked as if he wanted to say something more on the subject, when Dylan spoke up.

"Do these deliveries show up every place you appear?''

She nodded.

"For how long?'' Dylan asked.

Gina appeared suddenly, dressed in a flowing skirt that almost masked her limp. "They started six months ago.''

"What?'' Destiny gasped.

She watched as Gina lowered her gaze. "David and I thought it would be best if you didn't know about them."

"David's your manager?" The question came from the agent.

She nodded. "But if I get this pilot, I won't have to spend forty-five weeks a year traveling. Whoever's sending these silly flowers and cryptic notes will probably lose interest when he doesn't have to follow me all over hell's creation and back."

"Pilot?" Wesley asked.

"It could lead to some really terrific things for me, and David—"

"Wants to make sure he gets a financial piece of that action," Wesley finished.

She gave Wesley a reproachful look, then turned to the obviously less hostile Dylan. "David knows how hard I've worked for this."

"How long have you known him?"

Destiny did a mental tally before she answered. "Almost ten years. He owned a small comedy club in Maryland." Noting the skeptical expression on the agent's face, she formed the letter *T* with her hands. "Time out here," she said. "David has done nothing but wonderful things for me. He gave me a shot when I was only eighteen. He arranged for financial backing so that I could go out on the road to build a reputation. He—"

"Also wanted to be a comic, isn't that right?" Wes said.

Sighing, Destiny said, "That was years ago. David gave up on performing when he realized he didn't have the timing to do stand-up."

"So now he's living his dreams vicariously through your career?"

Glaring at Wesley now, she felt her blood pressure begin to rise. "As soon as you pass your boards, Dr. Porter, feel free to diagnose at will. Until then, I'd be grateful if you'd keep your Psych 101 diagnoses to yourself."

"It is a possibility," Dylan said, breaking the string of tension connecting Destiny to the handsome doctor.

"No," she said, without even a trace of the venom she'd spewed at Wesley. "The worst thing I can say about David Crane is that he can, on occasion, be overbearing."

"What about the other people you're close to?" Dylan queried.

"There's only Gina and Walter."

"Gina's the one with the gun," Dylan surmised, smiling at the now-demure Gina. "Who's this Walter person?"

"Walter Sommerfield," Destiny answered. "He lives in Potomac, Maryland. He and his daughter, Samantha, used to come to every one of my shows when I was working at David's place." Sadness settled over her as she remembered the bright-eyed young woman with so much promise. "After Samantha died, Walter sort of latched on to me and gave me the backing I needed to hit the road."

"What happened to the daughter?" Wesley asked.

"She died in a car accident two days after she was accepted at Harvard Law School. Walter had already lost his wife. Losing Samantha nearly killed him."

Wesley nodded. From anyone else, it would have been a comforting gesture. From Wesley, though, she interpreted it in a completely different way.

"Is Walter's pain psychologically significant?" she asked. Why, she wondered, did everything this man say or do annoy her so much? It was like nothing she'd ever experienced in her life. Destiny walked over to the phone, lifted it from the cradle and held it near Wes. "Maybe you can have a session over the phone. Maybe you'd find it fascinating to discuss the story of his only child's death?"

Calmly, Wesley took the phone from her hand and replaced it. In the process, his knuckles brushed against her skin, causing an immediate and involuntary reaction. It was a tingle that warmed her blood and quickened her pulse for just an instant.

"I have no intention of causing anyone any pain," he said softly.

When he spoke in that deep, velvety voice, Destiny was quite certain that she would do anything he asked. Hell, she thought, if he used that voice to tell her to take a leap into Charleston Harbor, she'd be smelling like fish and diesel fuel in no time flat.

"Tell me about the first delivery," Dylan said to Gina.

"She was onstage," Gina began. "I thought they might have been from her father, so I took a peek at the card. When I saw it—" Gina paused as a chill shook her body "—David and I decided to toss them. They've been coming like clockwork for the past six months."

"What's your first recollection?" Dylan asked Destiny.

Taking a seat across from the two men, Destiny didn't hesitate with her answer. "I received a pot of gardenias with *the note* when I was appearing in the Bahamas about three months ago."

"And you hired a detective to try and trace the deliveries?" Dylan continued.

Destiny met Dylan's concerned eyes and said, "Miller. Gina can give you his number."

"Why did you think the flowers were from her father?" Wes asked.

"Carl's like that. The pot was huge, you know. Destiny's father never does things in half measure."

Wesley's dark brows drew together. "And I guess you're sure he's not behind this? Meaning it as a joke," he added quickly.

"My father's an alcoholic who spends more time in detox than he does at home," she answered. "So even though he does have a slightly off-center sense of humor, he couldn't afford to do something like this, nor would he ever do anything remotely threatening to me."

There was something about the understanding she saw in Wesley's expression that made her feel suddenly less hostile and more willing to share with this man. Still, she wasn't yet able to let down the barrier of her stage persona. Donning a huge smile, she said, "In case you haven't noticed, it's politically correct and quite in vogue to come from a dysfunctional family." She leaned across the coffee table, her glass cupped between her hands. "My father's binges are well documented, and I even make references to them in my routines. It happens to be common knowledge. But *this*, this is another matter altogether."

Gina abruptly excused herself from the room.

A small alarm went off in Destiny's head. The two women were as close as sisters. It was very much out of character for Gina to run off like that. Then again, her little voice of reason argued, maybe Gina was hiding in case the matter of her father's current residence became a part of the conversation.

"And this Miller person you hired never found anything?"

"Nothing," she admitted, feeling silly for even paying his bill in light of his complete and total lack of results.

"Did anyone know you were coming into Charleston a day early?" Dylan asked.

"I think I said something about it when I was onstage the other night—in front of about two hundred and fifty people. Something about a one-day vacation."

"That narrows it down," Wesley said with a resigned sigh.

"Do you get these flowers every night? Opening night?"

"It varies," she told Dylan. "Sometimes I get four or five in a week. Other times I only get them on opening night. Once it was the last performance."

"No pattern," Wesley said to Dylan.

"They scare the bejesus out of me every time," Destiny said. "That's a pattern."

"Can you think of anyone who would want to hurt you?" Dylan asked. "Maybe you've gotten some weird mail, something like that?"

"You would have to ask Gina for—"

"What in the hell are you two doing here?"

Startled, Destiny turned toward the angry voice. She actually jumped when David slammed the door with enough force to rattle the watercolor prints on the walls.

Dylan and Wesley rose in unison, both men appearing unfazed by David's display of ire.

Wesley spoke first. "I'm Rose's son, Wesley, and this is Dylan Tanner. We dropped by to discuss the threats against Ms. Talbott."

David cast her an irritated look before turning his furious brown eyes on Wesley. "Anything even remotely connected to Destiny is my business. I'll handle everything—without interference from some bar hand and his buddy."

Dylan wasted no time producing his official identification. David visibly blanched.

"As far as I can tell," Wesley began, "you've done very little to protect Destiny from the individual who seems to be quite aware of her every move."

"I hired a detective!" David wailed in his own defense. "And he's never gotten close to her. He only leaves her notes and flowers."

"He got pretty close to her today," Wesley said. For the first time Destiny heard the faint trace of an actual, honest emotion in his tone. It could only be described as annoyance. For some reason, that pleased her. It also disturbed her.

"What are you talking about?" David thundered as he stomped over to her side.

"He left her a welcoming pot of gardenias at the Tattoo," Dylan stated.

"How in the world would he know you were arriving today?" David asked

David was her manager, accustomed to orchestrating every aspect of her professional life. She could tell by his narrowed eyes that he was struggling to control his fury. Apparently he wasn't too thrilled to have this Ivy League poster boy basically tell him to go to blazes.

"Destiny, baby, I'm sorry," David soothed. "We'll find out who's pulling this garbage. I know it scares you, but I'm sure it's just some sicko getting his jollies."

"Do we need your permission to look into all this?" Wes asked.

"Hang on," Destiny said to Wesley. "I'm the one who makes that decision. Try asking me." She stepped away from her manager.

"Fine." Wesley shrugged as he spoke. "Dylan has already done some preliminary work, which is why we came by at this late hour."

"Preliminary work?" she repeated. "What kind of preliminary work?"

"He made a few calls about Greg Miller, your detective."

Destiny met Wesley's eyes. "I wish I had known that. I'd like to ask that incompetent for my money back."

"That would be rather difficult," Wesley said.

"Bankrupt?" Destiny sighed as she lowered her gaze. Lord knew she'd watched her father file under one chapter or another through the years.

"Not exactly," Wes said as he moved to stand directly in front of her.

His tall body blocked her view of the others in the room. Gently he placed his thumb under her chin and applied just enough pressure to force her to meet his eyes. For what felt like an eternity, Wesley searched her face, his eyes roaming over every feature. She held her breath, somehow sensing that whatever he was about to say wasn't going to be good news. She was right.

"Greg Miller was found shot to death two weeks before you received that invoice."

Chapter Four

Destiny was still shaken by the news long after Dylan and Wesley had gone. She was also confused by the uncharacteristic behavior of the two individuals whom she considered her closest friends.

After Dylan and Wesley left, David explained that he had come crashing into the villa because he'd heard her scream from his room two doors down.

"Don't ever go into law enforcement," she teased him. "Not if it takes you the better part of a half hour to respond to what you think might be a crisis situation."

David blushed slightly. "I wasn't dressed," he defended lamely.

"Neither was I," Destiny said, closing her eyes at the memory.

"Those two just showed up here?"

"Right on the first guess." She sighed. "I certainly didn't invite them."

"I'll speak to Rose. I'll tell her we don't want her kid inter—"

"Please don't do that," Destiny interrupted. "And I'd hardly call *Dr.* Porter a kid."

"Then why does he still live with his mommy?" David retorted snidely.

Destiny regarded him for a long, quiet moment. He was really angry. Obviously he hadn't yet forgiven her for choosing the beach over the city.

Glancing up at the clock, she almost let out a groan when she noted it was nearly two in the morning. This was supposed to be the night she caught up on lost sleep. Instead, she knew she was destined to try salving David's rumpled feathers yet one more time.

Gee, she thought glibly to herself, *then I can wait a few hours and have my mother screeching in my ear for not following her directive.*

HER PREDICTION PROVED true when she got "the call" at precisely 8:45 the next morning.

And also true to form, Mona was furious. "Why is Carl still in jail?"

"Because he broke the law in some small town in Georgia?" Destiny asked sweetly, cringing when she heard the irritated sigh come across the line.

"I told your girl to have you handle it immediately."

"Gina isn't my girl," Destiny corrected gently. How could her mother have gone from Woodstock to snob in just one lifetime? she wondered not for the first time. "I got in late, but I plan to take care of the fine first thing."

"How could you have left him in some small town jail for the night?"

"I doubt he noticed," Destiny assured her mother. "They'll probably have to perform CPR just to get him out of the cell."

"Is everything a joke with you?" Mona asked.

Destiny heard the rustle of fabric and knew her mother was pulling on her judicial robes as the conversation progressed.

"I wasn't joking," Destiny promised her mother in a more respectful tone. "The charge was drunk and disorderly. If he'd been tossed out last night, before some of the alcohol wore off, I was afraid of what might happen."

Mona was silent for a second. "I suppose that was one way of handling it. But next time I'll consider calling Peace. Even though your sister and her husband struggle for every cent they have. Children are expensive."

"And Peace ought to know. That must be some kind of record, four kids in five years?"

"Your sister understands the importance of family."

"My sister needs to get a VCR or find some other way to spend her evenings."

"My clerk is calling," Mona told her in clipped syllables that fully and completely conveyed her disappointment in her firstborn child. "Can I count on you to handle this situation?"

"Of course you can," Destiny told her. "Have I ever let you down? Wait!" she quickly amended. "Don't answer that. Love you, bye."

"How is her royal nastiness?" Gina asked.

Destiny shrugged, sure her friend had heard enough of the conversation to understand the status quo between mother and daughter was basically the same.

"You look exhausted," Gina commented. "Do you want coffee now or do you want to try and get some more sleep?"

Placing her fingers over her tired eyes, Destiny knew returning to sleep wasn't a possibility. Visions of Wesley Porter had haunted her dreams, leaving her feeling oddly lonely in the first light of day. Her dreams, like most everything else about her, tended to be bold and vivid. The resplendent images of being locked in his strong arms had awakened her on more than one occasion during the night.

"Probably best if I start the day," she said as her feet hit the floor. "I sure hope my mother's call won't set the tone for the day."

"Maybe that cute doctor will find another lame excuse to drop in."

She looked up to find Gina staring at her, one brow arched toward her neat French twist.

"Meaning?"

"Are you telling me you aren't attracted to him?"

"I don't even know him," she said as she pulled on her robe.

"What's to know? The guy's gorgeous, friendly—seems like the perfect material for a short-term fling."

"I don't have short-term flings."

"Well," Gina persisted, "maybe it's about time for one."

"It's career time," Destiny insisted. "Once I've established myself, then I can think about a husband and a family."

Feeling Gina's hand on her shoulder, Destiny looked up into the sad, chocolate-colored eyes. "I didn't suggest anything permanent, necessarily. But don't keep kidding yourself, Destiny. You're counting on a future. Futures change. I'm an expert on the subject."

SLIPPING HIS GLASSES from the bridge of his nose, Wesley surveyed the flurry of activity from the shadows near the door. An appreciative smile tugged at the corners of his mouth as he admired her from a distance. That woman didn't need stage paint and glitter. "And she sure as hell doesn't wash out," he muttered.

"No, she sure doesn't."

"Hello," he said, tearing his gaze from the stage and glancing in his mother's general direction.

"Is everything all right?"

"I guess." Clipping his glasses into the front of his shirt, he allowed his eyes to travel back to the small woman cradling the microphone.

"I thought you were supposed to be studying," Rose observed.

"Just taking a break," he said defensively.

"Or have you decided to study the human body instead of the human mind?"

He gave his mother a sidelong look meant to quell the optimism he heard in her voice. "I was simply taking a break, and wandered in here for a couple of minutes."

His mother nodded but gave absolutely no other indication that she was convinced about his motives. "Shelby called, said she and Dylan were coming by tonight to catch the show."

"I'm sure they'll enjoy themselves. They haven't had much time together since Cassidy was born."

"I told them we'd reserve a table for six down front."

"Six?"

His mother patted her lacquered hair and averted her eyes. "I asked Destiny's manager and that woman Gina to join us."

Wesley swallowed the groan in his throat. "Her manager's a jerk."

"Is that a medical observation?" Rose teased. "Or personal, maybe?"

Wesley smiled at his mother. He knew better than to pursue this line of dialogue. Rose had made no secret of her desire to have a daughter-in-law and some grandchildren in residence at The Rose Tattoo.

"I've got to get back to work," Wes said.

"You can't do that," Rose told him.

"Why not?"

"Because I told Destiny you'd drive her home after they finish setting up all these lights and microphones."

"Why did you do that?" he asked, trying to sound perturbed, though the thought of spending some time alone with Destiny appealed to him much more than he was willing to admit—even to himself.

"Because I was under the impression that you were protecting her from whoever is sending her the flowers. Shelby told me that you've enlisted Dylan, as well."

"I simply asked him to give me an assessment of the situation."

"So that explains why you dragged him out to the beach in the middle of the night."

Wes felt his cheeks color.

"And—" Rose tapped her finger against his breastbone "—Shelby is *very* unhappy that you dragged her husband out in the middle of the night. But I'm sure she'll tell you all about it this evening."

"Great," Wes grumbled. "Maybe I'll skip opening night."

"Why would you do that?"

Wes spun and found himself staring down into those breathtaking violet eyes. "My mother got me into trouble with Shelby."

He watched, fascinated, when her lips parted and she blew a steady stream of breath upward, toward perspiration-dampened bangs. Her mouth was perfect. Her lips reminded him of sweet cherries—full and ripe. His mind flashed vivid images, all of which, he felt sure, would earn him a resounding slap from either Destiny or his mother. Or both.

He smelled good, she thought as she tilted her face up. And he was staring rather intently at her mouth. It shouldn't have bothered her, but Destiny's pulse increased when she noted the blatant curiosity as he scrutinized her features. Without even trying, Wesley had her nerves tingling with a very potent mixture of anticipation and expectation. As his blue-gray eyes traveled over her features, Destiny felt as if she was being caressed. It was unnerving.

"So," she began as soon as she'd placed a protective smile between herself and the doctor, "you'll be here tonight? I'm usually at my best on the first and last nights."

"Really?" Wes said, his head listing pensively to the left. "I'll try to remember that."

"Don't strain yourself," she retorted, meeting his amused eyes. "Gina said you invited her to join you this evening. Thank you," Destiny said to Rose. "She usually gets stuck backstage. It was very thoughtful of you to include her."

"Don't be silly. We'll have a lovely time."

She gave the woman's forearm a gentle squeeze. "Still, it was a very nice thing for you to do."

Destiny was a little surprised to see the woman's cheeks color slightly beneath the thick layer of blusher.

"I've got a few things to do back at my office. Wes will run you out to the beach."

"If you're in the middle of studying, I can take a cab. As I told Rose, it's not a problem."

She watched as his broad shoulders lifted in a shrug. "It's not an inconvenience."

She regarded him through the thickness of her lashes. "I don't believe you."

He met her eyes and said, "It *is* an inconvenience, but not nearly as inconvenient as the ramifications if I don't take you home."

"What?"

"If I don't take you home, my mother will rag on me for days. So you see, taking you home is a far superior option than incurring the wrath of Rose."

Destiny smiled. "Mothers are such fun, aren't they? I bet she had you on a guilt trip all through your childhood."

"I didn't grow up with Rose," he said quietly. "My parents were divorced when I was small. I lived with my father and stepmother."

"It looks like we have something in common, Doctor. My folks split up when I was five."

"Casualties of relaxed divorce laws."

"Is that what you think?" Destiny asked, her fingers automatically moving to his arm. His skin was warm beneath her touch. "Divorce was the best solution for my parents. I shudder to think what would have happened to all of us if they'd stayed together."

"Meaning?"

Her brow wrinkled at the clinical ring to his question. "My sister and I would have been the casualties if my mother hadn't left my father. He drank, they fought. Hardly a nurturing environment for children."

"You have a sister?"

"Peace," she said.

"Peace and Destiny?" he said, struggling to contain the snicker.

"Childbirth and LSD." Destiny sighed.

"No wonder your father is chemically dependent."

"He's a drunk," Destiny corrected. "I love him dearly in spite of it, so you don't have to worry about being so politically correct."

"I wasn't being politically correct," he asserted as his hand snaked around her waist.

Destiny could feel the warm indentation of his splayed fingers as he guided her out into the midday sun. She swallowed, hoping to quell the spark igniting in the pit of her stomach.

"Chemically dependent isn't politically correct?" she challenged. "Right."

"I meant it in the medical sense. If your father was attracted to drugs in his youth, he's probably an addictive personality. One sort of dependency usu—"

"I thought you weren't supposed to be studying now," Destiny interjected. "You sound like a textbook, Doctor. Lighten up."

"A textbook, huh?"

Destiny slipped on a pair of dark sunglasses and tried not to fixate on the feel of his thigh brushing hers as they walked slowly down the stone path to the parking area. It was like trying not to take a breath. Every cell in her body seemed to be aware of him on some level. Her mind honed in on every conceivable detail. The lithe movements of his body, the muscled strength of his thighs, the rather cocky assuredness of his swagger. She took in his profile from behind the safety of her glasses. He was certainly attractive, but that didn't explain her response. Wesley wasn't the first attractive man she'd encountered. *But he is the first* intelligent, *attractive man I've met,* her mind reasoned.

He held open the door of his car.

"This is yours?" she asked, cocking her head to one side as she stood next to the Mercedes convertible.

"Not bad transportation for a textbook, is it?"

Destiny snapped her mouth shut and scurried into the car. Why was Wes the one with all the punch lines? And why was she now adding financially stable to attractive and intelligent?

He slid behind the wheel, tugging at the knees of his faded jeans in one fluid motion. Destiny fumbled with the seat belt as he started the engine. She was just regaining her equilibrium, when Wes reached across her lap to open the glove box. His forearm pressed against her legs, rustling the flimsy fabric of her cotton dress.

"What are you doing?"

His answer came in the form of a sudden *pop,* as the forward edges of the convertible top were released. Wesley didn't right himself immediately. His hand dropped from the glove box, and his fingers wrapped around the contours of her knee. He was close enough for Destiny to be able to smell the fresh scent of his shampoo. Close enough for her to feel the urge to run her fingers through the thick mass of unruly dark hair falling forward into his eyes. Close enough for her to feel the heat emanating from his massive frame. Destiny went perfectly still.

He drew closer, until she could feel the warmth of his breath wash over her face. Quietly his eyes searched her face before he asked, "Any further developments from your fan?"

An involuntary shiver doused her budding passions the instant she thought of the creepy notes and flowers.

"Not a word."

Destiny should have commented when his hand slid from her knee to her waist, then over her arm and her shoulder, until she could feel his palm cup her chin. Where was her sharp wit? Surely she could think of some cute remark that would inspire him to take his hand away. She could, but she didn't want to.

She knew that for certain when she braved a look at his face. Concern seemed to temper his expression. She saw it in the deep lines beside his eyes and mouth.

"Are you okay?" he asked softly.

"Sure," she responded with false lightness as she pulled back from his touch. "I'm fine. I tried to tell you last night that I'm not letting this fruitcake get to me."

He frowned, apparently not buying her brave front. "He's getting to you. You're too smart to be so nonchalant about a potential threat."

"Gee," Destiny began, batting her lashes at him, "nice compliment. Sorta like 'That dress doesn't make you look quite so fat.'"

"You know what I meant," Wesley countered with a frown.

"I know," she said, softening her expression with a genuine smile. "But you're wrong about me."

"Really?"

"I'm not intimidated by this guy."

"Caution and intimidation aren't the same thing."

"I know," she said, winking in an attempt to lighten his mood. "I'm smart. Remember?"

"Then be smart enough to do whatever's necessary to find out why you're being stalked."

Destiny swatted his hand away and ran her fingers through her hair. "Please stop using the word *stalked*. And either put on the air-conditioning or throw back the top. I'm going to expire in this heat."

"Avoidance," he grumbled as he reached over and pressed something that made a whirring sound.

Blue skies, bright sun and a sweet-smelling breeze filled the car. "I'm not avoiding anything," she told him as he put the car into Drive.

"Uh-huh."

"I'm not." Destiny turned in the seat, tucking her leg beneath her in the process. Her eyes took in the strong angles of his face. Everything about this man seemed to exude strength.

"Whatever you say."

"I'm not," she insisted. "I'm simply not willing to allow some lunatic to dictate my actions."

"And what happens if this lunatic decides he wants to do more than just admire you from afar? Then what?"

"Are you trying to scare me to death?"

"No. I'm trying to get you to understand the potential danger of this situation."

"Why are you doing this?"

"Doing what?"

"Caring."

Wesley met her eyes briefly. "Don't most people care about you?"

"You answered my question with a question. You do that a lot."

"Sorry."

"My friends care about me, Doctor. But we're hardly friends."

"Really?"

"That's another question."

"Sorry." He raked his fingers through his hair. "Why aren't we friends?"

"We don't *know* each other," Destiny said with a little laugh. "Maybe we would have been friends. That isn't the point. I don't understand why you've made me your *cause du jour.*"

"You aren't a cause. You're a woman with a serious problem."

As she digested his answer, she wasn't quite sure whether she liked it or not. "I'm a woman used to solving her own problems."

"I'm sure you are," Wesley told her easily. "But there's no crime in asking for help. Especially when it's freely offered."

"Nothing in life is free, Doctor."

"Very cynical," he observed. "Care to expound?"

"Not particularly. Suffice it to say that I strongly believe that you have to pay for everything in one way or another."

"I believe you've just simplified the dynamics of karma into a cross-stitch sampler."

"Cute," Destiny remarked, feeling herself relax. "Beneath that professional exterior lives a wicked sense of humor."

"Don't tell anyone."

"Your secret is safe. Besides, I'm not keen on any more competition."

"Do you constantly look over your shoulder for the next shining star?"

Destiny smiled and captured her hair in her fist as the car accelerated out of the city. "I try never to look back. It isn't healthy."

"Are you always this evasive?" Wesley queried.

"I guess it's been a long time since I carried on a conversation with anyone other than Gina or David."

"Very limited. Too limited for such a beautiful young woman."

"Thanks, I think. You certainly are good at giving backhanded compliments."

"Sorry. Must be Rose's influence."

"She seems like a very nice lady. Very real."

"Except for her delusions about Elvis Presley and her passion for wearing animal prints."

"There's nothing wrong with a flamboyant personal style or an appreciation of the King."

"I agree. But I'll admit it was something of a shock to discover my mother looked and acted like a reject from some BBC comedy."

"What do you mean, *discover?*"

"I've only recently reestablished a relationship with Rose. Mostly because of my brother, J.D. He and his wife went back to Florida shortly after they were married."

"He's the guy who did the dependency?" she asked.

Wesley nodded. "He and Tory—that's his wife—had some trouble with the renovations."

"What kind of trouble?"

"They found a body shorn up in the wall."

"Yuk!" Destiny said with a groan. "Thanks for sharing that with me. It will make standing on that stage really comfortable."

"It wasn't a body, actually. It was a skeleton. And everything worked out in the end."

"Sounds peachy," Destiny managed to say. "Anything else you'd like to share with me?"

"I could tell you about Chad's kidnapping, but I'll save that for another time."

"Chad? Isn't that Agent Tanner's son?"

"Yep."

"Is The Rose Tattoo cursed, or something?"

"Nothing so sinister," Wes assured her. "Just a bad year or so for the locals."

"I guess if my admirer shows up, he'll be in good company here in Charleston. That's something."

"Calm down, Destiny. The guy in the wall was the former owner. And the Tanners' son was returned safely to his very grateful, albeit overly indulgent, parents."

"And everyone lived happily ever after," she said as they parked in front of the villa.

"Absolutely," he answered holding her door open.

"Then I guess I should feel relieved that I'm here."

"Maybe not," Wes said, nodding his head in the direction of the door to her villa.

"Great!" Destiny fumed as she spotted the large, crudely wrapped package guarding the entrance.

"Wait a second!" she heard Wesley call out. Determination and a fair amount of anger fueled each step. "I can't believe he found out where I was staying."

"I think we should call Dylan."

Destiny tore into the paper expecting flowers. But it wasn't flowers.

Chapter Five

"Don't touch it," Wesley instructed as he gathered her against him, his eyes fixed on the weird thing.

"Don't worry," she replied, her hands clutching the fabric of his shirt. "I have no desire to touch *that.*"

She remained against him while he dug into her purse, got her keys and led her into the villa. "We'll call Dylan, and I think we should consider calling the police."

"And tell them what?" she asked, tilting her face upward. "I've been down this road already. The authorities can't do anything until this fruitcake actually threatens me," she said as she pushed away from him and moved across the room.

He leaned against the counter as silent rage welled inside him. "What he did to that doll is somewhat threatening."

She shivered and ran her hands along the bared flesh of her arms. Her expression was guarded—only her eyes gave him an insight to her true feelings. What he saw in her eyes was a blend of fear and disbelief. Wesley intellectualized the disbelief, but his response to the fear was more primitive, more primal. Despite the inherent strength he sensed in Destiny, he also believed there was a fair amount of vulnerability buried beneath the surface. Not a helpless vulnerability, but a vulnerability born of determination.

"I don't understand," he said, stuffing his hands into the front pockets of his jeans.

She nervously twisted several strands of hair around one long, tapered finger. "I spoke to a police officer in Miami. They told me that until this guy does something more overtly threatening than sending flowers, there's nothing they can do."

"That's crazy!"

"That's the law," she told him with a sad smile. "Basically, this lunatic has to hurt me before the police can do anything."

"Maybe it's different here in South Carolina."

"I doubt it."

Wesley reached over and snatched the phone from its cradle. He punched numbers in stiff, irate succession. "Hello."

"Shelby, Wesley. Is Dylan around?"

"He's at the office. Why?"

"Destiny got another delivery."

"More flowers?"

"Not exactly."

"Then what?"

"A doll."

"Why does a doll have you so upset?"

Wesley turned his back on Destiny and cupped his hand over the receiver. "It wasn't the doll, really. It was what he did to the doll."

"Which was?"

"He painted the face to look like hers. There was a gardenia stuck onto one of the hands."

"Sounds sick," Shelby commented.

"My thoughts exactly." Wesley took a deep breath. "He left it at the villa. It's obvious he's watching her."

He heard Destiny's sharp intake of breath and instantly regretted voicing his suspicions aloud.

"DID YOU TOUCH IT?" Dylan asked as he squatted in front of the ghastly little trinket.

"No," she answered as her eyes sought Wesley. "I haven't played with dolls since I was a kid. And I'm not all that keen on playing with that one."

"Now can we call the cops?" Wesley asked his friend.

"We can, but it won't accomplish much," Dylan admitted, with an apologetic smile to Destiny.

"How can that be?"

Dylan shrugged as he rose. "Local law requires a definitive threat."

"What the hell does that look like to you?" Wes retorted.

"It's a doll, Doctor," Destiny explained in a soft voice. "Not a particularly flattering doll, but a doll, nonetheless. At best, the police will probably think it's nothing more than a tasteless gift from a fan."

"She's right," Dylan said as he placed a hand on the other man's shoulder. "The best we can do is alert them to the problem, arrange for Destiny to stay someplace safe and have someone with her twenty-four hours a day."

"Hold on," she interrupted, feeling ignored by the two men. "I can't just go into hiding. I have responsibilities, a club date. If I do as you suggest, this bozo wins. What kind of solution is that?"

Wesley and Dylan stared at her in obvious shock. Wesley spoke first. "You can't just pretend this isn't happening."

"Oh, yes, I can," Destiny assured him with a forced smile. "I won't allow *anyone* to jerk my chain like this."

"Be reasonable," Wesley cautioned. "While I can respect your need to retain some control over your life, it would be foolish to go on as if this wasn't happening."

Blinking, Destiny looked up into his eyes and silently wondered if he knew what he was asking of her. It simply wasn't possible. "It isn't just about me," Destiny explained. "If I go into hiding, what happens to Gina and David? Not to mention the fact that I don't have much more than a few weeks' worth of savings."

"This isn't about money," Wesley countered.

"Really?" she asked as she lifted her hand and began counting off on her fingers. "I have to pay Gina and David, as well as my own living expenses. My father's fines, court costs and requests for handouts come on a regular basis. My sister doesn't think a thing of borrowing money from me, so don't tell me it isn't about money. I have responsibilities. People that depend on me."

"They won't be able to depend on you if something happens," Wes argued.

Frustration swelled in her veins, bringing with it a surge of suppressed anger. "Nothing will happen to me," she insisted. "I've never done anything in my life that would make someone want to harm me."

"Apparently your admirer has a different opinion."

"Why are you doing this?" she implored, looking up into his troubled blue eyes.

"I'm not the one doing this," he explained in that even, calm tone that set her teeth on edge. "I'm only trying to make you realize that it doesn't make sense to assign rational motives to an irrational individual."

"You sound like a textbook again," she observed.

"But he's right," Dylan argued. "There's not much any of us can do for you until this guy shows his hand. Until then, it's probably a smart move for you to take precautionary measures."

"Precautionary measures for what?"

The sound of David's voice in her ear made her jump. So did the fact that she hadn't even heard him approach.

"And what's that?" her manager asked, pointing to the partially covered doll.

"A gift," Destiny informed him as she forced a smile to her lips. "It seems my creepy fan has discovered my hideout."

"Don't joke, Destiny," David warned as he rubbed his hand over the bristling growth of his beard. "How could this have happened?"

"Who knows?" Destiny answered vaguely.

"The villa is rented in the name of Tiffany Glass. How did he find you?"

"Wait a minute." Wesley jumped in. "If the villa is rented under an alias—"

"Tiffany Glass is the name Gina used when she wanted to hide during her modeling days," Destiny clarified. "Gina simply suggested we use that name in case the guy tried to send me flowers at home."

"How long ago did you make the reservations?" Dylan asked.

"Not until the day before we arrived," Destiny answered. "There was some ... discussion about where we'd be staying."

Dylan and Wesley exchanged confirmatory nods.

"What?" she asked.

"I think we'd better go back inside," Dylan suggested as he held open the door.

The group flowed into the cool interior. Destiny felt frazzled and out of control. The feelings reminded her of all those years she'd tried to be all things to all people. Dylan made a phone call while she filled the ice bucket and set out a tray of ice tea and glasses.

Destiny took a seat on the sofa. Wesley, who'd been standing over by the patio doors, came over and took the seat next to her. She caught the scent of his cologne and felt the gravitational pull as his large body settled next to hers. The resulting imbalance made her list toward him.

"Where's Annie Oakley?" Dylan asked.

"She's taking care of an errand for me," Destiny answered, a small smile tugging at the corners of her mouth.

"What kind of an errand?" David demanded, his eyes narrowing as he glared at her from where he sat across from them. "Don't tell me."

"It's just a fine and a few—"

"I thought we agreed that you wouldn't keep bailing him out of trouble."

Destiny felt her cheeks color as Wesley and Dylan stilled to listen to the exchange. "I don't think now is the appropriate time—"

"You promised me, Destiny," David bellowed.

"I did no such thing," she countered. "I did listen to your opinions on the subject."

"And you promised to heed my advice."

"I *promised,*" she began, stressing the last word, "to consider your position. I never said I'd turn my back on my father."

"He's a drunk, a leech."

David was on his feet, pacing the floor like a predator waiting to move in for the kill. Destiny noted Dylan was observing the situation with a bland expression. Wesley was another story. He'd leaned forward, his elbows resting on his knees. The action caused his shirt to stretch across the massive expanse of his chest, outlining the sculpted muscles beneath.

"And he's my father," Destiny reminded David. "I can't cut him off. Even if I did, my mother would go to Peace, then she would hit me up. It's easier to simply handle this myself, cut out the middlemen."

She caught Wesley's expression in her peripheral vision. He appeared quite interested in this public washing of her family laundry. "It's taken care of, David."

"Which means we can expect him in the next day or so," her manager concluded. David turned to Wesley and said, "Tell your mother not to let him into The Rose Tattoo. Destiny's father is an ugly drunk. He likes to pick fights he can't win and leave the penance for his daughter."

"It isn't like that," Destiny countered, though even she didn't fully believe her protest.

Wesley's hand moved across the couch cushion until his fingers closed over her knee. He gave her a quick, supportive squeeze. The warmth of his touch lingered long afterward.

"Tell me who knew where you were going to stay," Dylan asked.

Sighing, Destiny closed her eyes for a second as she performed a mental tally. "My mother, my sister, Walter."

"Walter Sommerfield?"

"Right." Destiny took a sip of tea. She watched as David continued to pace, certain he was trying to work through some of his anger. Destiny secretly longed for the simpler days back in Maryland, when David was his old jovial self. She wondered what had happened to the fun-loving man she'd known ten years ago.

"Would this Walter person have any reason to tell anyone where you're staying?" Dylan asked.

"Walter?" she scoffed, placing her glass on the table. "He would have no reason to tell anyone where I am. And besides, I'm not even positive he knows where I am. I haven't spoken to him since I arrived."

"He knows." David spoke up. "I called him just before we left Miami."

"Okay," Destiny said with a nod. "I'll call him and see if he's mentioned it to anyone."

Destiny dialed from memory and waited a short time to be put through to the prominent D.C. attorney.

"Hello, my dear." Walter's greeting was as warm and polished as ever. "How are you enjoying Charleston?"

"It's lovely," she told him. "But I've been getting those disgusting flowers here."

"Perhaps you should come home," Walter suggested, his deep voice full of concern.

"He sent flowers to me in Maryland, too," she reminded him. "I doubt I'd be any safer back there. Besides, I love working."

"We can hire security."

"We've been over this before," Destiny said, lightening her tone. "I don't want someone glued to me night and day. It would be too hard having a stranger around constantly. Besides, I have David and Gina with me."

"Gina is hardly protection against a madman, and David wouldn't be much better."

She heard a rustling of papers come over the line. "I've also managed to find myself a psychiatrist and an ATF agent," she explained. "You know how good I am at picking up strays," she teased, not wanting to alarm Walter. Dylan seemed to take her remark as intended, but Wesley frowned, apparently not thrilled with being compared to a wayward animal. "Anyway, we were wondering if you might have mentioned the location of my villa to anyone."

"Not a soul," Walter answered without hesitation. "Why?"

"The creep sent a delivery here today," she told him. "I think Agent Tanner was just interested in how this guy knew where to find me."

"He sent you flowers at the villa? Not the club where you're performing?"

"He's apparently expanding his horizons," Destiny said with a small, fearful laugh. "I just can't figure out how he knew about this place. I mean, I didn't even know until Gina showed me the brochure the other day. Also, we didn't cancel the hotel reservations until the day before we left Miami. Which means..." She paused for a fortifying breath. "He must have followed me or David. David's only two doors down.''

For the first time, Destiny was touched by the cold realization that someone close to her might be behind the torment. "I'm sorry," she mumbled into the receiver. "What did you say?"

"I asked if David was with you."

"He's right here."

"May I speak to him?"

Destiny extended the phone to David, but he didn't take it, opting instead to go off into Gina's room.

"Is he always so secretive?" Wesley asked, nodding in the direction of David's disappearing back.

Destiny shrugged. "He and Walter often have long, private conversations. They've been friends for years."

"Just what is Sommerfield to you?" The question came from Dylan, though Wesley seemed ready and eager to hear her reply.

"He put up the money to shoot a pilot for a sitcom."

"Just for the heck of it?" Wesley asked.

She smiled at him. "Right, the guy had nothing better to do with a few hundred thousand dollars. No, Walter has followed my career since I was eighteen. He saw me perform in David's club. He used to bring his daughter there all the time. Samantha had a real thing for stand-up."

"Samantha's the deceased daughter?"

Destiny felt her smile wane when she thought about Samantha. The girl had shown incredible promise. Samantha had been pretty and smart, and she'd had the sense of timing of a natural comic. If only she hadn't...

Destiny banished the memories with a shake of her head. "She and Walter came in regularly whenever Sam was home from school."

"And she died . . . ?"

"In a car accident," Destiny supplied. "She'd left the club, where apparently she'd been sneaking drinks on the sly. Her blood alcohol level was through the roof when she died."

"How did Walter take it?"

"Like you might expect," Destiny told Wesley. "She was his life since his wife died. He positively beamed whenever he talked about her. He was so proud that she'd gotten into law school. She was all set to go to Harvard at the end of the summer. Walter was positively devastated for months."

"So how did he hook up with you?"

Destiny reached forward and rolled the glass in her palms. "I think Walter just wanted to hold on to something his daughter loved. Samantha loved comedy."

"I thought you said she was going to practice law," Dylan observed.

"Walter wanted her to, and Lord knew she had the brains. But Sam probably would have been happier to polish her routine and hit the road."

"Wait a minute," Wesley said, waving his hands as if confused. "Sommerfield's daughter was performing at David's club?"

"She was good," Destiny assured him. "Better than good. She did this one bit where she sang a medley of country and rap tunes, called it crap. It was a stitch."

"How did her father feel about her wanting to be a comedienne more than a lawyer?"

"He never knew," Destiny admitted. "Sam was too afraid of disappointing him."

"Harvard Law is tough," Dylan remarked. "She was willing to go through three brutal academic years just to keep from annoying daddy?"

"I thought she was okay with it, you know?" Destiny said, her voice slightly tremulous. "I guess I was wrong."

"Why would you say that?" Wesley asked.

Destiny implored him with her eyes. "I should have seen the signs. After she died, the investigation revealed that Sam had been drinking heavily for a while."

"And you think you should have intervened." Wesley finished with a knowing nod.

"I should have sensed that she was really troubled. Then maybe she would still be alive and Gina wouldn't . . ." Destiny let her voice trail off.

"What does Gina have to do with all this?" Dylan asked.

"Nothing," Destiny said automatically. "She was just in the wrong place at the wrong time." Destiny looked directly at Wesley when she said, "Sam's car crossed the center line and hit Gina's car head-on at seventy miles an hour."

Chapter Six

"Is Gina's limp a result of the accident?" Wesley asked shortly after Dylan and David had left the villa.

"Yes. She shattered her leg." Destiny rose and tried to occupy herself by clearing away the glasses. "It cost her her career."

"Doing what?"

"Gina was a very successful model."

"That makes sense," Wesley said.

Destiny smiled. "She's very beautiful."

"And completely devoid of any self-esteem?"

Shaking her head, she allowed a small laugh to pass through her slightly parted lips. "I'll give you a dollar if you'll stop diagnosing for an hour."

His expression grew sheepish. "Sorry. Occupational hazard."

"I understand completely," she admitted. "Sometimes I have a hard time turning off the jokes, especially when I'm nervous."

Wesley moved closer, until she could see nothing but the vast expanse of his chest. He was nearly a foot taller, which required her to tilt her head back in order to maintain eye contact.

His gaze swept over her face, pausing to study each feature in turn. The sensation of being caressed came flooding back, causing a lump to lodge in her constricted throat.

"What sort of things make you nervous?" he asked in a deep, velvety voice that she felt all the way to her toes.

Destiny's eyes never left his face and she didn't blink. She was too afraid of breaking the electric thread connecting them.

"I'm uncomfortable around attractive shrinks."

He responded with a lopsided grin. "Is that a fact?"

"Yes."

Slowly he raised his hands until they cradled her elbows. On pure reflex she lifted her palms and flattened them against him. She felt the soft mat of hair beneath his shirt, along with the rapid, uneven beat of his heart. A little voice of reason began whispering words of warning. But she didn't listen.

Destiny knew that under normal circumstances she would never allow herself to touch a virtual stranger. However, she rationalized, in light of her current situation, taking the comfort Wesley was offering felt right.

"So, are you telling me that I make you nervous?" he asked as his hands moved higher.

"Yes."

"I don't think I've ever made a woman nervous," he continued as his hands worked until his fingers began a gentle massage of the tight muscles at the base of her skull.

"I find that hard to believe," she said, struggling to keep from closing her eyes. Wesley's hands were wonderfully relaxing and exciting at the same time. A small moan rumbled in her throat when his thumbs began tracing small circles against the sensitive flesh on either side of her throat.

She took in a long, slow breath, savoring his clean, utterly masculine scent. Cupping her face in his palms, he allowed his thumbs to move over her cheeks, as if he were committing the contours of her face to memory. The gentle pressure was as soothing as it was erotic, and she took an involuntary step closer, completely mesmerized by this man.

His hands stilled the instant her thighs brushed against his. Destiny started to move back.

"Don't," came the soft command.

"But you—"

"Shh," Wesley soothed.

His eyes fell to her open mouth, and he studied her lips for what felt like an eternity. The chime from the clock echoed in her ears as she held her breath. Waiting turned into longing in an instant. She acted on the longing.

Her palms moved over his chest, sculpting the solid muscle as she explored the contours of his body. It was as smooth and well defined as polished marble, but he emanated enough heat to assure her that he was anything but carved stone. Still, he made no overt move to kiss her. His restraint was something of a gauntlet—an intriguing situation, to say the least.

Destiny was all too happy to engage in this game with Wesley. She sensed that his control was the result of some chivalrous code, and that was blatantly exciting. It was also the main reason she was willing to become the aggressor. Somehow deep within her she knew he had relinquished total control of the situation to her.

Control. The word echoed in her mind until it finally got her attention. Destiny stepped away from him. When he showed absolutely no reaction, she knew for certain she had done the right thing.

"Fooling around with you would be a mistake," she said to him with characteristic candor.

"I wish you had told me that before I got all hot and bothered."

"You're a doctor, heal yourself," she suggested as she averted her eyes. "Besides, I know what you were doing."

"Fixing to kiss you?" he drawled in an exaggeration of his accent.

"You weren't *fixing* anything. You were manipulating me into a situation."

Wesley gave his chin a pensive stroke. "And just how did you come to that conclusion?"

Grabbing a handful of her skirt in each hand, Destiny braved meeting his eyes. "You're a take-charge kind of guy, yet all of a sudden you wimped out and encouraged me to play temptress."

"Is that what you think I was doing?"

She took in his innocent expression, but didn't buy it for a second. "C'mon, Doctor, I appreciate the sentiment, but we both know the only reason you staged this little scene was to illustrate to me that I'm still in control of my own life, in spite of the lunatic dogging my every move."

Wesley reached her in two long strides. His fingers closed around her arm, pulling her close to him.

"If that's what you think, you aren't as smart as I gave you credit for being."

ROSE WAS in her dressing room, admiring the tackle box full of stage makeup. Destiny was glad for the excellent ventilation system, since Rose had on enough perfume to leave a vapor trail. She silently chastised herself for thinking such an unkind thought about such a kind woman. She chalked it up to her foul mood. She chalked her foul mood up to Wesley.

"If you keep brushing your hair like that, you'll tear it out at the roots," Rose observed.

"You're probably right," Destiny admitted as she placed the brush on the edge of the vanity.

"Should I read something into the fact that you and my son seem to be sharing the same level of frustration?"

"Don't be silly," Destiny said, though she couldn't bring herself to meet the other woman's eyes. "Your son and I don't share anything."

"Except strong wills and an even stronger attraction."

Destiny gaped at the woman. "I don't know where you got that impression."

Rose tapped one saberlike red nail near her eye. "I've watched you two. You and my son were meant to be together. It's destiny."

"Yes?"

"No," Rose said with a shake of her head. The mound of teased hair didn't move. "I wasn't calling your name. I meant you were Wes's destiny. The woman he's been waiting for."

"I hate to tell you this, Rose," she said as she slipped behind the screen and pulled off her robe, "but your son isn't waiting for *any* woman, least of all me."

"Nonsense," Rose countered as she fell into the chair in front of the mirror and absently primped. "Wes wants a wife and kids."

"Wes? Or you?"

"Both," Rose answered without hesitation. "He just hasn't found the right woman . . . until now."

"I'm not the right woman," Destiny insisted as she pulled the zipper on her skirt. "And I'm just passing through."

"You're the one," Rose announced with all the confidence of the president delivering the State of the Union address.

"You're going to be disappointed, Rose."

"We'll see," she responded before she slipped from the room.

Destiny was surprised the find a simpleton grin on her lips. "Why am I smiling?" she asked her reflection. "Rose is obviously nuts."

"And what makes you think that?"

"Hi, Gina," she said as she watched the tall woman ease through a small crack in the door. "Rose is under the mistaken delusion that there's something between Wesley and me."

Gina nodded.

"Well?"

"Well, what?" Gina asked as she began to organize the cosmetics back into the tray.

Destiny snorted and continued to fiddle with her hair. "You're supposed to say 'That's crazy' or 'Gee, Destiny, where'd she get an insane notion like that?'"

"I can't do that." Gina sighed. "I think she may be right."

"*What?*"

"I think Dr. Porter is perfect for you."

"Gina!" Destiny yelped. "Have you lost your mind? The next thing I know you'll tell me you're the one sending the flowers and that god-awful doll."

Gina's expression grew solemn. "I would never intentionally do anything to hurt you."

Destiny reached over and caught the other woman's wrist. Their eyes met in the lighted mirror. "It was a joke," she said, punctuating the remark with a gentle yank on Gina's slender arm.

The other woman's smile didn't reach her cautious brown eyes. "It wasn't funny," Gina replied with a pout.

"I'm sorry." Destiny let her hand fall away, but she kept her friend in her line of sight. "Don't be mad, Gina. I really am sorry if I offended you. I'm only joking about the flowers because if I don't . . ."

Gina's expression softened and warmed. "I know. You've got to be scared out of your wits."

"Let's hope not," Destiny retorted with an exaggerated wink. "I've got a show to do."

HE WOVE THROUGH THE CROWD just as she was coming onto the stage. Anger caused sweat to coat his face in a sheen of clammy moisture. And it was all her fault, he thought as he took his seat. His eyes zeroed in on her mouth as he ordered his drink from some faceless woman. Pure hatred darkened his eyes.

The waitress was back with his drink in a relatively short period of time. "The service is better than the seats," he grumbled as he pulled several damp bills from the front pocket of his trousers.

The waitress ignored his dig. That only made him more furious. He was in no mood to be ignored. Especially by a lowly waitress. He brought the glass to his lips as he listened to the audience applauding her. They were morons.

When she smiled it made him want to stand and scream. Instead he took another long swallow of his Scotch, savoring the warmth it produced in the pit of his stomach.

He was being so patient. Mother would like that. She liked everything to be planned. She would be proud.

As he followed Destiny's movements across the stage, he noticed the tall black woman seated at the table down in front in the corner. That should have been his table. He'd called and reserved it. His anger was building to a barely contained frenzy. What was she doing in his seat? She was Destiny's flunky. She had no right to his seat.

He downed the remainder of his Scotch in one swallow and turned his attention back to his target. He ran the morbid filmstrip in his mind, over and over, as she played to this room full of blind fools.

He couldn't wait to hear her beg for her life. He was getting more and more anxious with each performance. He wasn't sure how much longer he could wait.

Fixing his eyes on her, he was careful not to reveal any emotion, especially with that other one sitting just a few feet away. Were they on to him? Did they know? He felt panic grip him. He needed to calm down. He began to stroke the knife inside his jacket pocket.

"...MY LAST DATE." Destiny paused and took a sip of water from a glass she'd placed on the stool. "He was so backward that his family still wasn't using fire." A small rumble of laughter came out of the void created by the bright spotlight. "He had so much hair on his back that I'm convinced his grandfather dropped from a tree limb. Thanks very much. You've been a great audience. Good night."

Destiny bounced off the stage and went directly to her dressing room. The happy, carefree smile she'd worn during her routine came off with the layers of makeup and the short, tight skirt. Something was nagging at the fringes of her consciousness. Something she couldn't quite define.

"Probably just all that nonsense about me and the doctor," she mumbled as she tugged her top over her head and twisted her hair into a knot at the nape of her neck.

"What about you and me?"

Destiny looked up to find Wes standing backward in the doorjamb. "I'm decent," she told him.

His presence filled the small space, making her feel trapped. "You're also very talented."

"Thanks," she said, averting her eyes.

"You seem upset," he observed as he took a single step forward. "Did you get another delivery?"

"No," she answered quickly. "I'm just in a weird mood. It happens sometimes after I perform. I'm sure it has something to do with a plummeting adrenaline level."

"So this is a biochemical funk?"

Destiny smiled and peered up at him through her lashes. "Do you always have to give an official-sounding label to everything?"

Wesley's chest puffed up before he defended himself. "I'll have you know that *funk* is not a generally accepted medical term."

"Point," she conceded. "But biochemical stands out."

"Point," he mimicked with an infectious smile. "My mother is springing for a midnight dinner. She told me to come and collect you."

"I don't usually eat this late at night."

"Neither do we," Wes told her. "So I think we're both bright enough to figure out that my mother is orchestrating this in the hopes that we'll find lasting and eternal love."

"Very good," she observed dryly. "I take it your mother has done this before?"

"Not to me," he said, raising his hands. "But she did a number on my brother."

"What kind of number?"

"She forced him to marry a woman under false pretenses."

Destiny cocked her head to one side and looked up at him. His eyes glinted with an amused light. "You're joking, right?"

"I swear." He made a cross over his heart.

"Incredible," Destiny said on a breath. "But what makes you think she's set her sights on fixing you up with me? Not that it's going to happen, mind you."

"She told me so," Wesley answered in a flat tone as if he might be commenting on the weather.

"At least she isn't devious," Destiny said.

"Oh, yes, she is," he said with conviction. "Don't turn your back on her for a second."

Destiny was smiling when she and Wesley emerged from the backstage area. Gina, David, Rose, Agent Tanner and a willowy woman with dark hair were waiting for them.

"That was delightful," Rose said just before she placed an air kiss in the vicinity of Destiny's ear. "It's so refreshing to hear a comedienne who doesn't resort to bathroom humor."

"I see where you learned the fine art of giving compliments," she whispered to Wesley. "Thank you," she said to her hostess.

"I'm Shelby," the tall woman said. "I understand you've already met my husband," she added with a searing look in Wes's direction.

"Nice to meet you." Destiny shook the woman's hand.

"I meant what I said," Rose said as she took Destiny's arm and led the pack. "The last time I saw Elvis in Las Vegas, he had a comic as an opening act. That young man didn't have half your talent." Rose's expression grew dreamy. "Of course, I barely remember anything but the way Elvis sang 'Can't Help Falling in Love.'"

"I doubt that," Wes said over her shoulder. "I'm sure you remember everything about your final encounter with the King."

Rose gave her son a warning look as they walked along the path to the rear of the restaurant. "Pay him no mind," Rose grunted. "He's too young to have any real appreciation for what a great man Elvis was. Why—" Rose stopped to allow her son to open the door "—Wesley's never even seen Graceland."

"I have," Destiny said.

"Really?" Rose chirped, her voice filled with an almost childlike excitement. "What did you think?"

"It was incredible," Destiny admitted, choosing her words carefully. "One of the most interesting things I've ever encountered."

"You're welcome to come with me in January."

"My mother makes a pilgrimage on his birthday," Wesley observed.

"I think that's nice," Gina stated. "I saw Elvis when I was young."

The meal included a continuation of the discussion on the king of rock and roll. Even David admitted to having been a fan, though he'd never carried it to the point of obsession, like Rose. Destiny was having a hard time staying with the conversation, but it had nothing to do with the topic. She was simply entranced by the Tanners.

Shelby and Dylan appeared to be incredibly smitten with each other. They were always touching. A hand here, a kiss there. It made Destiny wonder what it would be like to have such a close personal relationship with a man. Shelby seemed so happy. And Dylan was positively taken with his beautiful wife. They stopped looking at each other only long enough to discuss their rambunctious son and brand-new daughter.

"Are you okay?" Wesley whispered against her ear.

Destiny's heart rate increased tenfold as his warm breath washed over her exposed skin. It caused a tingling in the pit of her stomach.

"I'm fine," she told him.

"You still look upset. Are you telling the truth? You really didn't get another delivery?" he pressed.

Everyone at the round table went still. The only sounds in the room came from the jukebox and a log crackling and hissing in the fireplace. Destiny could hear her heart beating in her ears when all eyes turned on her.

"*Did* something happen?" Gina asked.

"No," she insisted. "I just got a weird feeling when I was onstage."

"What kind of weird feeling?" David asked.

"I don't know," Destiny said, feeling silly for having even brought it up.

"Tell me about it," Wesley prompted.

"When I was onstage, I felt like I was being watched."

"You were," David grunted. "By a full house of paying customers."

Destiny sent him a withering look. "Not like *that*. I mean that creepy feeling everyone gets now and then."

Shelby reached across the table and placed her hand over Destiny's. "Do you think it might just be because you got that horrible doll this afternoon?"

"Maybe," Destiny admitted, though she still couldn't erase the lingering doubts from her brain.

"He was there," Gina said, taking a nervous sip of wine.

"Where?" Destiny asked.

"Who is 'he'?" Wesley demanded.

Destiny's eyes pleaded with her friend, but Gina had a different plan. "There's this guy who's been coming to almost all of Destiny's club dates for the past few months. A real loser."

"What?" Dylan, Rose and Shelby barked in unison.

"It's not like she's making it sound," Destiny began as she ran the tip of her fingernail around the rim of her coffee mug. "He's just this pathetic little guy. He looks harmless."

"So did Son of Sam," Wesley noted.

"I can't believe this!" David said before pounding his fist on the table and scraping his chair on the hardwood floor. "Why didn't you say something before now?"

"I told that private detective!" Destiny responded in her own defense.

"I can't believe you've been this dishonest with me." David continued his tirade.

"I haven't been dishonest," she insisted. "I don't think he's behind all the deliveries, so I didn't want you to worry."

"I'm supposed to worry about you," David snapped. "It's my job."

"You can quit," Wesley suggested. There was a subtle, but definite, challenge behind the soft delivery of the words.

"Wesley Porter," Rose admonished.

There was a long moment of silence before David tossed his napkin on the back of his chair and stomped from the room.

"And I thought it was the talent that was supposed to be temperamental," Destiny quipped to the group.

"What has gotten into him?" Gina asked. "He's had a chip on his shoulder for weeks now. I'm glad he left, though. Now I'll be able to enjoy this scrumptious dessert without his surly face glaring back at me."

"Gina," Destiny said between clenched teeth.

Her friend lifted her head and blinked. "What? I'm tired of his nasty attitude. And I won't pretend otherwise."

"David doesn't deserve to have his character assassinated in front of others," Destiny said pointedly. "I'd better go and see what I can do."

"I'll go with you," Wesley said as he hustled to his feet.

"That isn't necessary," she insisted.

"It's probably a good idea," Dylan said. "I don't think you should be roaming around alone after dark."

"Yes, dear," Rose added. "Take Wesley with you just to be on the safe side."

"Fine." She relented, knowing if she continued to argue she'd probably miss David. "But hurry, and don't antagonize him anymore."

"Yes, ma'am."

"And don't ever suggest he quit again. I need David."

"Yes, ma'am."

"And give me an opportunity to talk with him in private."

"Yes, ma'am."

"And please stop that ma'am stuff."

"Okay."

She traced her steps back through the kitchen. A small group of people were involved in various stages of cleanup. The smell of grease hung in the air. It was also all over the floor, if the slippery feeling on the soles of her shoes was any indication.

Destiny reached the door, pulled it open and very nearly fell over David's unconscious form.

Chapter Seven

"Oh, no," Destiny cried as she dropped to her knees. Small pebbles dug into her flesh as she began to check her friend for injuries.

David groaned as she gently turned him over and placed his head in her lap.

"What happened?"

David's eyes opened as his hand began to massage his jaw.

"I happened."

Destiny's head snapped up as she searched the shadows for the source of the familiar voice. "Dad?" she called out.

Carl Talbott stepped into the light, cradling a pot of gardenias in one arm. A broad grin split his weathered, wrinkled face.

"How's my girl?"

"What have you done?" she croaked, her eyes darting between the flowers and her father's expectant expression.

Carl's gray eyebrows drew together. "He attacked me."

"Crazy old fool," David grumbled as he sat up.

"I'm neither crazy nor old," Carl stated unequivocally.

"But the flowers..." Destiny began as she rose.

Carl's expression softened as he thrust them out to her. "I brought you a little something. Just to say thanks for...uh...lending me a hand."

"You?" she gasped. Her eyes moved from her father to Wesley, then back again. "You've been sending me these?"

Carl's head fell to one side. The action caused his thin gray ponytail to flip onto his shoulder. "I, um..."

"You slime!" David shouted as he lunged at the older man.

Wesley intervened, catching David in midair before he was able to get to her father. "Hold it," Wesley barked as he locked his arm across David's throat.

"What's everyone so upset about?" Carl asked.

"Like you don't know," David rasped.

Wesley gave him a warning jerk. "Knock it off, Crane."

"He hit me," David argued.

Destiny's eyes widened as she gaped at her father. Carl had the good sense to look contrite, even going so far as to toy with a pebble near his booted foot.

"You hit him?" she asked.

"He came at me," Carl whined in his own defense. "I was only protecting myself."

Destiny turned to her manager. "Why did you attack my father?"

"I caught him with the flowers," David reasoned as he tugged against the restraint of Wesley's well-muscled forearm. "I guess I went a little nuts when I found him slithering around out here just waiting to scare the sh—"

"That's enough," Wesley interjected. "I think we'd better take this party inside."

Destiny sighed loudly and pressed her fingers against her temples as she walked. Confusion pounded in her head, drumming all sorts of thoughts through her brain. What was her father doing with a pot of gardenias? It wasn't possible.

Inside The Rose Tattoo, she almost winced when she saw the bright red splotch on the left of David's jaw. It was already swelling, and promised to evolve into a nasty bruise.

Of course, the bruise wasn't half as nasty as David's temper. The man was positively glowering by the time they marched in to the stunned group sipping coffee.

"What on earth?" Rose panted as she sprang to her feet.

"My father doesn't work and play well with others," Destiny said under her breath.

"It wasn't my fault," Carl insisted.

"More flowers," Dylan observed.

"Can't a father bring his daughter a little sign of affection in this state?" her father asked with great hauteur. Carl moved next to her and placed a kiss against her forehead. Again he tried to hand her the flowers.

"I don't want them," Destiny said stiffly.

Carl pursed his lips as he reluctantly placed the pot in the center of the table. In what seemed to be the same action, he grabbed a wineglass and reached for the bottle.

Wesley's large hand clamped on Carl's wrist as he said, "That can wait."

She could see the defiant light in her father's blue eyes and she silently said a prayer. *No scenes, please.*

"Carl, isn't it?" Wesley asked.

The two men stood toe-to-toe, which gave Wesley a distinct advantage. He was a good six or seven inches taller than her wiry father. Still, Carl wasn't exactly known for his self-restraint.

"Who the hell are you?"

"Wesley Porter. My mother—" he inclined his head in Rose's direction "—owns this place."

Carl slowly removed his hand from the wine bottle. "Nice place," he commented.

As soon as she heard the cordial tone of her father's voice, Destiny expelled the breath she'd been holding. If Carl was feeling generous, it was a sure sign that he hadn't been drinking.

"Would someone mind telling me what's going on here?" Rose asked. "What happened to your face?" she asked David.

"He did," David said with a pout.

"You shouldn't have attacked me," Carl piped up.

"Children," Destiny grumbled, "please stop." Brushing the strands of hair off her face, Destiny looked from David to her father. "Stop bickering and tell me what happened."

"I spotted him out back," David began through thinned lips. "When I saw the flowers, I went after him."

"And I've got great reflexes for a man my age," Carl said with a satisfied smile.

"How can you do this to your own daughter?" David yelled.

"Do what?" Carl countered. "And why are you yelling at me?"

"Dad," Destiny began, placing her hand on her father's arm, "tell me about the flowers."

Carl's expression changed again. This time he took on the appearance of a repentant child. "I was only trying to do something nice for you."

"Where'd you get them?" Destiny asked with a shaky smile.

Carl cleared his throat, then admitted, "I found them."

"Where?"

"Out back. Propped up on the tan car."

"What about a card?" Wesley asked.

"I tossed it in the bushes out back."

"You shouldn't have done that," Destiny told him.

"Why?"

While Destiny filled her father in on the mysterious deliveries, Wesley and Dylan went out in search of the card.

"Think he's telling the truth?" Wesley asked Dylan as he turned on his flashlight.

"Probably. He seems harmless enough."

"Unless he's your father," Wesley said with a frown.

"The guy is a little off-the-wall."

"That's putting it mildly," he said. "A gray ponytail and a silver peace symbol hanging around his neck. Someone ought to tell that guy the social revolution of the sixties has ended."

"I think he knows," Dylan observed dryly. "I just don't think he cares."

"You're probably right on target."

"I think I've got it," Dylan said as he dropped to one knee in order to reach beneath the branches of an oleander bush. "Right here," he said, holding the white rectangle in front of the flashlight beam.

"I can send it for prints, but I don't think that'll prove too useful."

"What's that?" Wesley asked, flicking a small shred of paper with his fingertip.

He held the light while Dylan turned the envelope in his hand. There, stuck under the corner of one staple, was a torn bit of cardboard. "What is it?"

"It looks like a portion of a business card." Dylan traced the small edge of a flower petal with his fingertip. "It might give us a lead on the shop that delivered these."

"Destiny told me they'd never seen a delivery truck." Wesley felt his pulse quicken with the thought that they might have discovered a significant piece of the puzzle.

"Well, maybe we'll get lucky with this."

"Dylan." Wesley grabbed the other man's arm. "Don't say anything about this to Destiny's manager."

One of Dylan's dark eyebrows arched upward in a question. "Want to tell me why?"

Wesley shrugged. "We both know that whoever is behind this has to have his hand on her pulse. Until we know who it is, I don't think it's a good idea to share this little development."

"And your money is on the manager?"

Wesley shrugged. "Everything seems to point to a man being behind this."

Dylan eyed him with keen interest as he continued. "Think about the threats—they scream masculine to me. Flowers, notes, the doll. They all fit into the category of things a man would give a woman."

"Unless the woman is a real sicko."

"True," Wesley admitted as a heavy weight settled on his shoulders. "We can tell Destiny when she's alone, but I think it would be better if we kept this to ourselves for the time being."

"Your call," Dylan responded. "I'm just wondering why you're going out of your way to help this woman."

"I'm a nice guy."

"Not that nice."

"Gee, thanks," Wesley grumbled. "What's wrong with looking out for one's fellow man?"

"Nothing," Dylan assured him. "Especially when that fellow man happens to be a beautiful woman."

"Good point." Wesley was smiling by the time they rejoined the others.

"Did you find it?" Destiny asked him.

He looked down into her brilliant, troubled eyes and felt his blood surge with an unmistakable urge that had nothing to do with flowers or notes. "Yep."

"Is it like the others?" she pressed.

Dylan carefully slipped his finger under the flap and removed the card. "Identical," he said.

Destiny lowered her eyes, and he swore softly under his breath. His hand moved to her shoulder, and he gave her a small squeeze.

"I'm spooked," Gina said. "How about taking us home?"

"I think you might want to move out of the villa," Dylan suggested. Come on into town where you're not so isolated."

"This is getting out of hand," David commented. "I'm only two doors down from them."

"I noticed your quick response time last night," Wesley taunted.

David bristled as a red coloring seeped up over his collar. "You've got a lot of nerve, Doctor."

"I'll stay with them," Carl suggested.

"We'll be fine," Destiny said, though Wesley wasn't sure whom she was trying to convince, the group or herself.

"Do you really think that's a good idea?" Shelby implored from across the table. "I've had some experience with your garden-variety lunatic, and I think you should consider doing as Dylan says."

"She's right, Destiny," Gina announced. "There's no sense in taking any chances. We can move our stuff into town. You know what they say about safety in numbers."

"Carl and I can keep an eye on you," David argued.

"Is this fan of yours really dangerous?" Carl queried.

Wesley wanted to deck the man. It was blatantly obvious that he was more concerned for his own safety than his daughter's. Watching the people in Destiny's life was a wonderful education for Wesley. No wonder she felt such an immense responsibility for everyone. They reminded him of hungry bacteria attacking a cell—draining the life from it, and leaving it open to a host of other predators.

"Don't worry, Dad," Destiny said with obvious forced lightness. "Gina has a gun."

"You can't be serious!" Carl gasped. "You have a gun with you when you know how dangerous they are?"

"Not if you're the one standing behind the barrel," Gina noted.

Carl wagged his finger as he raged on. "Statistically, you're probably going to be shot with your own weapon. Most of the guns used in street crimes came into the possession of the criminals when they were stolen from law-abiding citizens."

"My father's a strong advocate for gun control," Destiny said with a wry smile. "He also saves whales, marches for more stringent motor vehicle emissions, wants you to have your pet spayed or neutered, and eats only dolphin-safe tuna and pesticide-free vegetables."

"Don't you make fun of me," Carl warned.

"I'm not," Destiny assured him with a smile. "I think all your causes are admirable and they all have merit."

"That's the very reason this country is on a downslide," Carl argued. "Your generation doesn't care about the natural resources of this planet. You only care about making money."

"And it is my understanding that her money is what bailed your drunken butt out of jail this morning," Wesley observed darkly.

Carl visibly stiffened at his calmly delivered comment. Wesley felt the full force of the other man's barely controlled anger.

"My daughter was simply assisting me," Carl said. "She knows that as soon as my next book is published, I'll pay her back."

"Right," Wesley said with disgusted breath. "At any rate, your publishing prospects don't change the situation. She should move as soon as possible. One gets the upper hand on a stalker by outsmarting him."

"Are you some sort of expert?" Carl challenged.

"I happen to have some training in the behavioral sciences."

"From tending bar?" Carl sneered.

"From a medical degree with a specialty in psychiatry. I did my residency at St. Elizabeth's in Washington, D.C. I worked extensively with the criminally insane."

"Did I forget to mention that Wesley is a doctor?" Destiny sweetly queried.

"A doctor?" Carl repeated as he blinked, then nodded. "Good choice, my dear."

"Hold on," Destiny cautioned. "I didn't choose Wesley. He sort of came with the territory."

"Doesn't matter. He's a whole lot better than that loser your sister married."

"I am not marrying him, Dad. I'm working here for six weeks."

"We'll see," Carl responded, humming.

Wesley hid a smile behind his hand.

"ARE YOU SURE YOU'LL BE all right?" Wesley asked.

He stood silhouetted in her bedroom, leaning one shoulder against the wall. Moonlight cast bluish highlights through his straight, ebony hair. She could barely make out his face, though she could tell from the sound of his voice that he was frowning.

"I'll be fine. Dad and Gina are downstairs. David can be here in…half an hour or so, depending on how loudly I scream."

"I hope you'll reconsider and move downtown. At least then you wouldn't be a sitting duck."

Destiny let out a breath as she sat on the edge of her bed. "What's to say he wouldn't find me downtown?"

"Lots of things," Wesley said as he moved into the darkened room. "Your safety will depend on how many precautions you're willing to take."

"Such as?" she prompted, bracing her hands against the mattress by her sides.

She heard his small sigh as he gingerly sat next to her. Her hands kept her from falling against him. Heaven knew her common sense wouldn't. She was too aware of him, too interested for her own good. Everything about this man drew her attention—the sinewy feel of the corded muscles she felt where his thigh rubbed hers; the lock of hair that seemed determined to fall into his thickly lashed eyes; the blunt, square tips of his long fingers; those incredibly sexy eyes behind the intellectual-looking frames of his glasses. It was as if every nerve in her body received an electric charge from just looking at him.

"Why are you so stiff?"

"Stiff?" she repeated.

"You're very nervous."

"I told you," she said, her voice breaking. Then, after clearing her throat, she added. "You make me nervous."

"Me?" he asked in a low, seductive voice. "Or men in general?"

"Loaded question," she admonished.

"Honest question. Tell me."

Destiny lifted her face to his and met his eyes. "You."

"That's got some potential."

"For disaster," she quipped. "I told you this afternoon. This isn't a good idea."

"Says who?" he asked as his hand wrapped around her waist.

"Me," she told him without much conviction.

His fingers traced the faint outline of her spine, slowly inching up her back until she could feel him fumble with the pins in her hair.

"I don't believe you, Destiny," he said in a voice that was like liquid velvet.

Slowly, deliberately, he pulled his glasses off and set them on the nightstand. Destiny felt the pins slide from her hair, only to be replaced by the feel of his fingers entwining in the falling mass.

"It feels like silk," he murmured against her forehead.

The feathery touch of his lips against her skin coiled fire in the pit of her stomach. A small moan rumbled in her throat.

"This really isn't such a hot idea," she told him, though her tone lacked the force of her words.

"Yes, it is," he assured her. His hands cupped her face, angling it beneath his.

She watched him through wide, expectant eyes. Torn by the strong pull of attraction against her tense thread of self-control. The pads of his thumbs traced magical circles against her cheeks, coaxing her lips apart. His eyes seemed to darken with the unmistakable spark of passion.

He shifted them in one agile motion, so that the next thing she knew she was lying on the bed with Wesley at her side. His head rested in his bent arm, while he used his free hand to arrange a halo of hair around her face. She lay still, completely enraptured by his actions. His large hands were infinitely gentle as he reverently ran his fingers through her hair. Destiny longed to reach out and touch, yet didn't dare for fear she might break the spell.

His expression didn't change as his fingers stroked the sides of her face. She found the only indication of his reaction in the subtle change in his breathing. His chest rose and swelled with each sharp intake of breath, straining the fabric of his shirt.

She felt her lashes flutter against her cheeks as she stifled a groan. "I don't think I can take this," she told him in a shaky voice.

"Sure you can," Wesley promised.

She would have argued further, except words failed when she felt the warm tip of his thumb caress her lower lip. It was an infinitely gentle action—a slow dragging meant to entice. It wasn't until he increased the pressure that she realized it meant much, much more.

His own lips parted and his eyes remained riveted to her mouth as his slow movement gradually increased in tempo. Destiny could feel the last traces of her lipstick melting beneath his touch. He increased the pressure more, causing a friction that threatened to make the rest of her melt, as well.

"Wait, I—"

"Not this time," he said. "I don't think I'll give you the chance to talk me out of it."

He moved again, until one of his legs meshed with hers. The weight of his thigh pushed her deeper into the mattress. But it was the rigid hardness of his body that caused her to suck in her breath. He took handfuls of her hair, and his mouth loomed just a fraction of an inch above hers.

"I think you're an incredibly beautiful woman," Wesley told her in a husky whisper.

"Thank you," Destiny whispered. "I think—"

"Don't think," he implored. "I don't want you to do anything but feel."

"I feel," she assured him with a throaty laugh. "You must weigh three hundred pounds."

"Sorry," he gushed as he instantly reversed their positions.

Destiny found herself sprawled on top of him, fully aware of every inch of his strong body. Her palms rested against his chest, trapped between their bodies. The rapid beat of his heart echoed the deafening sound of her own.

The clean, masculine scent of his skin was at odds with the rough shadow of a beard she felt when his cheek brushed hers.

"Is this better?" he asked against her ear.

"Better than what?"

His hands closed on her shoulders and he regarded her for a long moment. "You're not going to make this easy, are you?"

She smiled down at him. "Nope."

"That might cause me to use more drastic tactics."

"Like what?"

"Like this," he said as he guided her mouth down, closer to his. Wesley stopped just short of making contact, fanning the heat of passion that was building between them.

The expectation was almost more than she could stand. Desire, fierce and palpable, spiraled in the core of her being. Reason swam against the strong current of attraction. She studied the angles of his face visible in the soft light of the room.

"Are you going to kiss me?" she asked when she could no longer stand the wait.

"Do you want me to?" he asked huskily.

"Yes."

"Good answer," he groaned as he raised his head.

And then his mouth was on hers, probing, persuading, awaking her body in ways she'd never dreamed possible. Her nails dug into the solid muscle of his chest as his tongue teased the seam of her lips. A moan reverberated in her mouth as he deepened his kiss.

His strong fingers raked through her hair, then moved lower, molding her against him—leaving no doubts about his need.

Destiny was reeling from the awakening of suppressed emotions. She felt as if she couldn't get enough. As if she needed the feel of his demanding mouth more than she needed her next breath. He began a slow rhythm with his tongue that literally curled her toes.

His palms slid over her back to her waist, leaving behind a trail of pulsating awareness. Destiny was doing a little exploring of her own. She massaged the hardened planes of his upper torso, fully conscious of the effect she was having. He spread his legs, cradling her softness between his powerful thighs, leaving nothing to the imagination. She could feel the extent of his arousal, and that knowledge brought with it a heady sense of power.

Wesley's fingers circled her waist, pulling her against the unmistakable hardness pressing into her belly. She heard several explosions and marveled at the fact that this man could inspire such an intense reaction.

"What was that?" he asked against her mouth.

"Fireworks," Destiny answered, glad he, too, had experienced the sensations.

Wesley rolled her off him and left her alone with her stunned expression.

"I don't think so," he said.

The alarm in his voice filtered through her passion-laden brain. "What is it?"

She had barely got the question out when she heard the rapid succession of pops again. It took a second for the sound of glass shattering to register.

"Stay here!" Wesley barked as he grabbed his glasses and moved to the door.

Destiny had barely managed to scramble off the bed when he disappeared down the darkened hallway. With her senses now fully functional, she began to process what was happening.

The unmistakable scent of gunpowder filled her nostrils as she followed the path Wesley had taken. She heard nothing above the pounding of her pulse. It was an eerie kind of silence, punctuated only by her raspy breathing.

Then she heard Gina's scream.

Chapter Eight

Acting on a rush of adrenaline, Destiny abandoned caution and raced for the stairs.

"Stay down!" Wesley yelled as soon as she appeared on the landing.

Dropping to her knees, Destiny scanned the dark room. Shadows cast by fingerlike palm leaves scraped the walls. She saw a flicker of movement out of the corner of her eye. "Wesley?" she whispered.

"Over here," he replied. "Stay down behind the sofa while I go and check on your father and Gina."

"Wait!" she yelled, crawling in the direction of his voice. "I want to come with you."

Moving on her hands and knees, Destiny made it to the bar, where she found Wesley crouched like a protective animal.

"I think it would be better if you stayed put."

"But I—"

His fingers gripped the tender flesh of her arms. He gave her a determined shake. "Those were gunshots we heard. Stay here while I check things out."

"I'm coming with you," she stated, prying his hands from her arms.

"At least stay behind me," he said, relenting after brief consideration.

Destiny followed him, careful to shield herself behind furniture whenever possible. It felt as if hours had passed before they reached the door leading to the guest room her father occupied. The stench of gunpowder was more pronounced in this part of the villa. It hung in the air alongside her unvoiced fears. The distant whine of a siren grew closer as she watched Wesley reach up and turn the knob.

It was then that she noticed the large, dark holes in the walls and the plaster dust beneath her hands and legs. "Someone shot at the house?" she asked.

"Carl?" Wesley called as soon as the door squeaked open.

There was no reply.

Forgetting any potential threat to her own safety, Destiny dashed passed Wesley and bounded into the room. She stopped at the end of the bed and took in the motionless form of her father.

A small, horrified sound came from her open mouth. She was frozen, unable to react to her brain's urgent message to go to his aid.

Luckily, Wesley didn't suffer the same debilitating paralysis. In no time he was at her father's side, lifting the man's limp wrist between his thumb and forefingers.

"He's got a pulse," he told her in a flat, decisive tone that reminded her he was a doctor. "I'm—"

Carl snorted.

It was a familiar sound that brought Destiny a flood of relief, followed by a squall of temper. "He's smashed, not shot," she groaned in disgust. "I can smell the bourbon from here."

"Let's check on Gina," Wesley said. "I don't think he'll notice we're gone."

Gina's room was on the opposite side of the hall— the side closest to the street. Wesley led the way, guiding her by the wrist. The hallway was now illuminated in red and blue strobe lights, and the sirens suddenly died outside the door.

"The police must be here," she yelled.

"Stay with me," he said as he opened Gina's door. "Gina?" he called out.

Foreboding filled her the instant she saw the odd angle of her friend's bent leg. It was an unnatural position, obviously not lost on Wesley.

"Oh, Lord," she heard him mutter as he reached the head of the bed, carefully sidestepping what appeared to be a knife. After checking Gina's pulse, he dropped her hand and reached for the lamp on the nightstand.

Destiny sucked in a breath and swayed when she saw the dark red stain on the front of Gina's robe. It was just below her rib cage and slightly off to the side.

"What should I do?" she asked.

Wesley slipped the gun from Gina's hand at the same time he began basic triage. "Go get the cops. Tell them to call the paramedics."

"Is she alive?"

"Yep," he said without ever looking up. "But she won't be if you don't hurry."

Destiny ran toward the door, sheer force of will all that was keeping her from panicking. Police cars lined the parking lot, and several officers in bulletproof vests were crouched behind the open doors of the vehicles.

"We need an ambulance!" Destiny yelled.

The next few minutes went by in a blur. Destiny stood with her back against the wall while Wesley barked orders to the officers and tended Gina's wound until help arrived. She felt helpless and useless, especially when she watched them bring in the stretcher. Closing her eyes, she ran her hands nervously over her arms. She could vividly recall the ugly wound and the black-handled knife on the floor.

"Miss Talbott?" asked a tall man in a crisp uniform.

"Yes."

"I'm Sergeant Greavy. I'd like to take your statement."

Destiny blinked up at him. His boyish expression softened as he gently led her into the living room and nudged her into a chair.

"Is Gina going to be all right?"

"I don't know," he said as he took the seat across from her and turned down the radio clipped to his shoulder. He pulled a small pad from his pocket and prepared to take notes.

"What happened here tonight?"

Destiny was distracted by the loudness of David's voice outside the villa. "He's my manager," she told the officer.

He smiled apologetically and said, "We can't let people in here just yet. He'll have to wait for you outside."

"He won't like that," Destiny commented.

"He doesn't have a choice. This is a crime scene."

A shiver crept along her spine.

"What happened?"

Destiny's eyes fell to the polished chrome nameplate pinned to his uniform. "There were some shots.

Gina screamed. We found her like that when we came downstairs.''

"We?"

"Dr. Porter," she explained. "We were upstairs."

"Doing what?"

Her blush was her response.

Sergeant Greavy cleared his throat and studied his pad. "Did either of you hear anything?"

Destiny shook her head. "Not until the gun went off."

"Did you hear any voices? Shouting? Doors opening? Anything like that?"

"Nothing," she told him. "Nothing at all."

Destiny jumped up from the chair when the paramedics wheeled Gina down the hall. A blanket covered her to the chin and a mask had been placed over her nose and mouth. Destiny rushed to the stretcher, careful not to disturb the plastic tubing from the IV's.

"You're going to be fine," she whispered. Tears filled her eyes when Gina failed to respond. "I'll stay with you," she promised.

She felt a hand at the small of her back. She didn't have to turn and look—she knew instinctively that it was Wesley. Odd that she should recognize his touch. Even more strange was the comfort she felt from his presence.

"Let them take her," he said against her ear. "Her vital signs are stable and I'm pretty sure the knife missed her major organs."

"Really?" Destiny asked, turning so she could see his eyes.

"Really," he repeated with a small, compassionate smile. "I stopped the bleeding without a whole lot of trouble. That's a good sign."

Destiny breathed a sigh of relief and rested her cheek against his chest. "I can't believe this happened."

"Excuse me," Sergeant Greavy said, "but I'd like to get your statements before you go to the hospital."

Wesley led her back into the living room and sat with her on the sofa. He took her hands, folding them into his own. Destiny noticed the stains on his shirt and felt her stomach turn. "Thank God you were here," she said, giving his hand a squeeze. "There's no way I could have dealt with this by myself."

"You owe me one."

"Dr. Porter," the police official began, "Miss Talbott said the two of you were on the second floor?"

"Yes, we were," he answered.

"And what did you hear?"

"Two loud bangs. Then gunshots, a scream and then more gunshots."

"And was it the victim you heard screaming?"

"It was Gina," Destiny answered. It made her very uncomfortable to hear Gina referred to as a victim. It seemed so cold, so impersonal.

"I gave one of the officers Gina's gun. She was still holding it when we found her," Wesley said.

"So you think the victim was firing at the perpetrator?"

Destiny nodded. "Gina was pretty quick to draw her gun."

"What about the guy in the other room?"

"My father," Destiny stated. "He drank himself to sleep from the looks of it."

"We'll have to question him," Greavy said.

"You'll want to wait until he's . . . uh . . ."

"Sober," Destiny finished for Wesley.

"I see," said Greavy. "He'll have to leave here so that the crime investigation unit can come in."

"What am I going to do with him?" Destiny asked. "I promised Gina I'd be at the hospital."

"I'll cart him down to David's," Wesley offered.

"Really?" Destiny asked. "That would be great. Except David probably won't think so."

"Is David the guy outside with the lungs?" the sergeant asked.

"He doesn't like to be excluded," Destiny explained. "Can we go now? I really don't want Gina to wake up in some strange hospital alone."

"In just a minute. Do you have any idea who might have wanted to harm—" He flipped through his notepad in order to finish his question. "Miss Alverez?"

"No one," Destiny answered. "Gina doesn't make enemies."

"But Destiny does," Wesley told the officer. He then spent the next several minutes recounting the six-month history of the stalker.

"And you have no ideas regarding his identity?" Greavy asked.

"Not a clue," she admitted. "And I gave all the notes to the detective I hired in Miami."

"We'll contact him," Greavy said with a nod.

"He's dead," Wesley explained.

Greavy appeared positively fascinated when Wesley told him all about the oddities surrounding her creepy fan. He even went so far as to suggest Sergeant Greavy speak to Agent Tanner regarding fingerprints and some scrap of paper.

"What was all that about a business card?" she asked as Wesley hoisted her father's limp form over his shoulder.

"I was going to tell you," he said. "Grab the door," he instructed.

They were careful not to disturb the small group of men and women measuring and photographing the spray of bullet holes. As they moved down the hall, Destiny again focused on the bloodstains on Wesley's clothing. It was a sobering reminder of the evening's events—not that she needed any reminders.

After dropping her father at David's, Wesley escorted her to his car and they headed for the hospital.

"Thank you for what you did for Gina," she said as she turned to take in his handsome profile illuminated in the soft glow of the instrument panel.

"I'm just glad I was there to help."

"Me, too," she admitted, twisting her trembling fingers in her lap.

Wesley reached over and covered her hands as he said, "Don't worry. She'll be fine."

"I hope so."

"Her vitals were stable and the wounds don't appear to be life threatening. David's vitals went through the roof when I turned your father over to him. He looked primed for a stroke when I left him ranting."

"Did the paramedics tell you about Gina?"

Wesley chuckled. "I'm a doctor, remember?"

"You're a shrink."

"But I still had to go through medical school."

Destiny felt her cheeks warm. "Sorry. I guess I just never thought of you as a real doctor."

"Gee, thanks."

The warmth spread from her face to her neck. "I didn't mean it like that. I just think of psychiatry as a different kind of medicine."

"It is," he assured her. "But diseases of the mind can be just as deadly as diseases of the body."

"Our late-night visitor proved that," she said, closing her eyes as her mind started running through the possibilities. What if he'd killed Gina? What if he'd come up the stairs and found her with Wesley? What if he'd killed them all?

"You're thinking what could have happened, I'll bet."

She regarded him through her lashes. "We could all be statistics right now."

"But we aren't."

There was something immensely comforting in the conviction she heard in his voice. It was also reassuring to feel the warmth of his touch. Destiny closed her eyes, drawing on the innate strength of the man behind the wheel.

"I wonder if Gina will ever forgive me."

"What makes you think she'll blame you?"

"Wouldn't you?"

"No," he answered. "You can't control the actions of others."

"But I should have followed your advice. If I'd only insisted we move out of the villa immediately, Gina wouldn't have been hurt."

"That's possible," Wesley conceded. "But Gina's a big girl, and I don't remember you chaining her to the house."

"But if it weren't for me . . ."

"Gina wouldn't have a job."

"Or stab wounds," Destiny stated with a sigh.

"Don't beat yourself up," he told her. "Gina doesn't impress me as the type to hold you responsible."

It was Destiny's turn to chuckle. "You'd lose on that count, Doctor. Gina tries not to blame people, but deep down I think she's very, very angry over the way her life's turned out."

"The accident?"

"That accident cost her everything she'd worked years to achieve."

Wesley pulled the car in to the lot next to the hospital. Destiny followed him into the entrance next to the emergency room. When he reached down and took her hand, she was amazed at how natural it felt. She was also amazed at how easily she was allowing this man to orchestrate things.

"I'm Dr. Porter," he told the uniformed woman behind the admitting desk. "We're here about Gina Alverez."

The woman flipped through a small stack of folders. Extracting one, she clipped a form to the outside edge and slid it across the desktop. "Fill out sections A and B, and I'll need a copy of her insurance card for the files."

"She doesn't have insurance," Destiny stated.

The information was greeted with a definite frown, followed by an exasperated look.

"But I can guarantee payment," Destiny added, concerned that Gina would not get the appropriate care otherwise.

"Do you have a credit card we can imprint?"

Destiny fumbled through her wallet until she found her card. "I can cover all her expenses."

The woman gave her a look that fairly screamed her disbelief before she disappeared into an area behind her desk.

"I wonder what's happening," she said to Wesley, her eyes moving to the closed doors leading to the treatment areas.

"She's probably being given something for shock, something for pain and then they'll suture her wounds before admitting her."

She looked up into his eyes. "I never knew how beneficial it could be to hang out with a doctor. It probably would have taken me hours to get that information from the staff."

He smiled and winked playfully. "I do have my uses."

Destiny lowered her eyes and reminded herself that this man had enough charm for ten men. Charm she apparently was helpless to resist, if her behavior in the bedroom had been any indication.

The memory of his mouth on hers brought an odd tingling to her lips and a warmth to the pit of her stomach. The man could kiss, that was indisputable. She'd about melted right then and there. She also couldn't help but wonder what might have happened. How far would she have allowed it to go?

"Thank you," the woman said, bringing her back to the present.

"I guess I passed the credit check," Destiny grumbled under her breath. "What would they have done if my card had been maxed out? Refused to treat her?"

"Probably," Wesley admitted as his hand pressed against the small of her back. He shrugged and said, "Medical care costs."

"Did you learn that in medical school?" she queried. "Or did you figure it out all by yourself?"

"I'm a bright guy," he answered.

"Really?"

He paused and looked down into her wide, teasing eyes. "I was bright enough to get you into bed in less than twenty-four hours."

"Ouch," she groaned. "And just for the record, you didn't get me into bed."

"You have a different name for that thing with the mattress and box spring?"

"For your information," she began with her spine stiff and her head held high, "we were on the bed, not in it. And you weren't getting any farther than a kiss."

"Wanna bet?" he purred against her ear.

Destiny fought the urge to slap his conceited face. She simply scoffed loudly and pretended there was no possible truth to his statement.

"Put your testosterone away," she told him.

"Not a chance," Wesley promised with a lopsided grin. "At least, not while you're close enough to smell the soap on your incredibly soft skin."

"Stop saying outrageous things," she insisted, battling to counter the effect of his words on her pulse.

"There's nothing outrageous about the truth," he stated. "All I have to do is close my eyes and I can still feel the outline of your—"

"Stop it!" she whispered. "This is a hospital. My friend is gravely injured and all you can think of is your...is..."

"Making love to you?"

"Sex," she hissed through clenched teeth. "Complete strangers don't make love."

"Speaking from experience?"

"I'm not going to dignify that with a response."

"Because you're not speaking from experience," he concluded with a very satisfied smirk.

"No comment."

"No need." He sighed. "Your eyes give you away, Destiny. You've never made mad, passionate love to a man."

"I'm not a vestal virgin saving it for marriage, Doctor."

"Good," Wesley said as his arm moved up until his hand draped over her shoulder. "I'm not patient enough to be anyone's first time."

"This is an absolutely pointless conversation," she grumbled as she shrugged away from his touch. "Your arrogance is annoying."

"It isn't arrogance, Destiny."

"Could have fooled me."

"It's simply the fact that I recognize our mutual attraction and don't choose to fight it."

"You're insane," she said with a mirthless laugh. "I'm not attracted to you."

"Is that why you kissed me?"

"*You* kissed *me*."

"Want me to do it again."

"No."

"Liar."

Destiny expelled a loud breath and began counting to ten silently. She had gotten up to seven when they reached the waiting area where someone was supposed to update them on Gina's condition.

It was a small, rectangular room littered with cups and fast-food wrappers. It smelled faintly of stale coffee and citrus deodorizer. The seating consisted of a tattered plaid sofa and some vinyl-covered chairs with metal frames. Destiny opted for one of the uncomfortable chairs.

Wesley fell onto the sofa, crossing one long leg over the other, his hands laced around his kneecap.

"I'm sorry about your shirt," she said after a long, unnerving silence.

"It's nothing."

"It's ruined. I'll be happy to replace it."

His expression took on an edge. His eyes clouded and narrowed and his lips pulled into a taut line. "I'm not your responsibility, Destiny. I don't need anything from you."

The sharpness of his tone stiffened her spine defensively. "I was simply being polite."

"No, you weren't. You're too used to claiming responsibility for anything and everything."

That rankled. "At least I can handle responsibility."

One dark brow arched upward. "You think I'm not responsible?"

"I think you live with your mommy and you have no job. Hardly a long list of accomplishments for an adult man."

She had hoped her barb would put him in his place. Instead, he seemed very amused by her assessment of his character. "So, you don't like me because of my living arrangements?"

Destiny rolled her eyes in frustration. "I didn't mean that."

"Then you do like me?"

"I didn't say that, either."

Wesley uncrossed his legs and leaned forward. "I don't live with my mother. But then, you'll see that for yourself as soon as we leave here."

"What's that supposed to mean?"

"I'm taking you back to my place."

Chapter Nine

"When pigs fly," she informed him.

"Do you have a better plan?" he asked.

"I can check in to a hotel, just like Dylan suggested."

"Except that Gina won't be with you. You'd be alone. After what happened this evening, I would think you would want company."

"Company?" she repeated. "You're a lot of things, Wesley. But good company isn't one of them."

"I like that," he said with a smile.

"Being insulted?"

"I like the way my name sounds on your lips."

"You," she stammered as she got to her feet, "are incorrigible. Can't we have a conversation without some pathetic attempt to seduce me?"

"Pathetic?" he parroted. "I've never been called pathetic before."

"There's a first time for everything," she assured him.

Wesley rose slowly and moved next to her. He bent his head and placed his mouth next to her ear. She could feel the warmth of his breath as he spoke.

"That's what I'm hoping for."

"You're like a dog with a bone," she said, giving him a small shove backward. "Get off it, please?"

"For now," he agreed quickly.

Too quickly, her mind noted.

"Miss Talbott?" a man dressed in surgical scrubs asked as he entered the room cradling a metal clipboard in his arm. "I'm Dr. Alred."

"Destiny," she corrected, feeling a burst of fear flow through her as she took the hand he offered. "How's Gina?"

He nodded and offered a kind but tired smile. "She's going to be fine. She's on her way to surgery."

"Surgery?" Destiny managed to repeat over the lump in her throat.

"We have to take care of a minor internal injury. She'll be in the OR less than an hour."

"Internal injury?"

Wesley reached for her, folding her against his body. "They need to go in and suture all the blood vessels to prevent later complications," he explained.

The doctor looked up from the page and eyed Wesley curiously.

"I'm a doctor," he explained.

"Then I guess I don't need to tell you all about the procedure," Alred said as relief washed over his haggard features. "She'll be out until tomorrow morning."

"I still want to stay," Destiny insisted.

"I'm afraid Sergeant Greavy left strict instructions that she wasn't to have any visitors. In fact, he's posting a patrolman at her door."

"Oh, God," Destiny groaned as she turned against Wesley's chest. "This is all my fault."

"No," Wesley assured her as one hand stroked her hair and the other rubbed her back. "You had no way of knowing the guy would come after you."

"He's been warning me for months," she whispered into the shirt she had balled in her fists. "It should have been me."

"You're being ridiculous," he said. "It shouldn't have been anyone."

Dr. Alred promised to have the staff contact her the minute Gina awakened the next morning. After much convincing from Wesley and the doctor, Destiny gave in. Wesley led her from the building with his arm wrapped tightly around her shoulder.

"They'll take good care of her," he said as they reached the parking lot. "It's a good facility."

"I still feel like I should stay here."

"You heard Alred," he reasoned. "Even if you hung around, they wouldn't let you see her."

"I can't believe the police would keep me away."

"They probably don't want you and Gina to compare stories until they've had a chance to investigate."

"What?" she cried.

They reached the car and Wesley turned her so that her back was against the cool finish of the Mercedes. Cupping her chin with his fingers, he lifted her face to his. "Don't take it personally. The cops have to guard the integrity of their investigation. At this point, all they know is that a woman was stabbed and that there were three other people in the house at the time."

"They can't possibly suspect my father," she said. "He was barely conscious when we carted him to David's."

Wesley smiled. "David didn't appear too thrilled when you told him he was going to be chief cook and bottle washer."

"He'll live," Destiny assured him. "I couldn't very well leave him there."

"The cops offered to take him to detox."

Tilting her head, Destiny glared at him. She caught her own reflection in the lenses of his glasses. It was a chilling sight. Her hair was disheveled and there was a telltale redness around her mouth. Automatically she raised her fingers to her lips.

Wesley followed her action with his eyes. "You do look thoroughly kissed."

"I'm a mess," she mumbled. "Why didn't you say something?"

"I just did."

"THIS IS WHERE YOU LIVE?" she asked when they parked in front of an impressive high rise on the banks of Charleston Harbor.

"My brother leased it when he was here. I simply took over the lease."

If the plush carpet in the lobby was any indication, Wesley Porter was living well. An elevator with polished brass railings deposited them on the seventh floor. Destiny followed him in stunned silence as he entered the apartment.

"I thought medical students ate canned spaghetti and were in debt up to their eyeballs."

"Some are," he said as he flipped on a wall switch, flooding the room with light.

"But not you?" It wasn't really a question, and Wesley didn't bother to respond. They entered a kitchen that reminded her of something out of a magazine. Bleached marble countertops sported trendy accessories, like a cappuccino machine and the very latest in kitchen gadgetry. The place was spotless, right down to a complete lack of water spots in the sink.

"Do you actually live here?"

"Yep," he answered as he moved to the sink and tugged his shirt from the waistband of his jeans.

Destiny's eyes grew wide and she swallowed as he shrugged out of the shirt. Her attention remained riveted on the deeply tanned flesh covering his well-muscled torso. "Diet Coke time," she mumbled appreciatively as her eyes scanned the rippling muscles at his waist. A mat of dark curly hair covered most of his upper chest, then tapered and disappeared into his pants. When he turned to the sink she saw he even had those incredibly sexy dimples on either side of his spine, just where the faded denim clung to his trim hips.

"There's soda in the fridge," he said as he turned on the faucet.

Destiny tried not to watch as his strong hands began to scrub the now-soapy shirt in the sink. She tried not to notice the way his muscles flexed and corded with each tiny movement. She just didn't try hard enough. At least, not until he looked over his shoulder and caught her staring.

"Want me to take the rest of my clothes off?"

"No," she squeaked, wincing when she heard the high-pitched sound come from her own lips.

"Too bad." He sighed as he turned back to washing the stains from his clothing.

"I can't stay here," Destiny said as she fixed her eyes on a bright red teapot decorating one of the burners.

"Sure you can," Wesley said without turning to her. "There's no way your fan can get up here. The building is secure, and you need a passkey to even get onto the grounds."

"I still think I should get a hotel room. Or I can call David and he'll put me up."

Wesley shut off the water, dried his hands on the front of his pants and leaned up against the counter, his arms crossed in front of his chest. His eyes met and held hers.

"You can't stay with David. I'm sure your fan knows full well that he's at the villas. A hotel might give you some measure of protection, but you'd be alone. You'd also be spending a ton of money unnecessarily. Here," he began, arching his arm dramatically, "you are safe, you have company and I won't charge you an arm and a leg."

Destiny regarded him for a long, silent minute. "What *will* it cost me?"

"That depends."

"On what?"

"On you."

HE FOLDED THE BLANKET over the sheet and finished making the sofa into a bed. Wesley kept glancing over his shoulder to check the closed door. He no longer heard her moving around in his bedroom. He should have taken heart in the fact that she'd fallen asleep. She certainly needed the rest. Instead, he found himself wondering what it would be like to be sharing that bed with her. Their kiss earlier in the evening had given him some indication. In spite of her aloofness, he'd sensed fierce passion, tasted suppressed desire on her lips.

"Maybe she's just lonely," he whispered into the shadows as he stepped out of his jeans and tossed them onto the nearby chair. It was a sobering thought. And one he'd never had before. He'd never questioned a woman's motives before. He'd simply taken whatever was freely given. Thanks in large measure to his looks, Wesley had been given more than his fair share in his thirty-two years. Especially after adding M.D. to the end of his name.

He punched the pillow and then raked his hands through his hair. "What am I doing?" he asked the shadows. Silence was the only answer.

SHE WAS STILL TRYING to figure out just what he'd meant when the sun peeked through the vertical blinds covering the large window. Destiny rolled onto her side and hugged the pillow to her body. Inhaling deeply, she found a strange delight in filling her nostrils with his scent. It clung to the sheets and pillows, surrounding her like a lover's arms.

"Where did that come from?" she asked her brain as she shifted into a sitting position. "What?" she yelped as she read the numbers on the bedside clock.

Destiny flew out from beneath the covers and ran into the bathroom. A bathroom, she noted, that had Jacuzzi seating for six. Utilizing items from a basket, Destiny showered and washed her hair. The complete lack of makeup was regrettable, but then, she didn't have an option. Nor did she have an option when it came to wardrobe. After braiding her damp hair, she reluctantly pulled on her rumpled dress and peered at her reflection in the mirror above the dresser. It wasn't great.

Her gaze dropped to the top of the dresser. There was nothing particularly personal. No keys, no scraps of paper, nothing that gave her any insights into her host.

"He's neat and organized," she admitted. "I guess that's something."

Three sharp knocks sounded on the door.

"Come in," she called before nervously wiping her hands along the sides of her dress. He looked incredibly sexy with his hair all disheveled, no shirt and no shoes. It summoned all sorts of images to her mind, several of which made her blush.

"You should have gotten me up earlier," she said as her foot toyed with the nap of the carpet.

"The hospital called."

Her head snapped up. "Is Gina all right?"

"She's fine," he answered quickly, leaning his large body casually against the jamb. "The doctors took care of three bleeders and they'll release her in a few days."

"Bleeders?"

"Leaking vessels and arteries nicked by the knife."

"You sound like a textbook again," she teased, offering him a small smile.

"I like to be exact." He shrugged.

"Have you ever taken care of bleeders?"

"A few times."

"When?"

His head tilted to one side and he adjusted the rims of his glasses. "Curious about me?"

"Just making polite inquiry," she stated.

Wesley snapped his fingers. "Shucks, I was hoping a night in my bed had—"

"Can I have a cup of coffee before we start sparring?"

"Sure thing," he answered, pushing himself away from the wall. "How do you take it?"

"Black," she answered.

The apartment was even more impressive than she had first thought. There was a huge living room with a breathtaking view of the harbor. Destiny stood next to the French doors, looking out at Fort Sumpter. Tourists appeared as mulling insects, navigating the stone wall of the national monument. Several shrimp boats dotted the horizon, as well as a few pleasure boats.

Destiny turned when she heard him enter the room. He carried a steaming mug of coffee in each hand.

"Black," he said as he extended one of the cups to her.

"Thanks. And thanks for letting me stay here last night. I'll make other arrangements today."

His frown reached his eyes. "I thought we covered all this last night."

She nodded and moved over to sit on one of the overstuffed chairs. It was white like the walls and the carpet. The only color in the room came from the paintings and the few ornamental items scattered about. Destiny couldn't imagine living in solid white, not with her predisposition to tracking in mud and sloshing coffee. She was very conscious of the stain potential as she held the mug with both hands.

"I know we talked about it, but I just don't feel right staying here."

"Where else will you go?" Wesley countered. "You need someone with you."

"I had three people with me last night and he still managed to get in."

"That villa was a bad idea. Dylan and I told you that at dinner. It was very open and exposed on two sides. Any incompetent idiot could have broken in."

Destiny set the mug on the glass coffee table. "But this wasn't an incompetent idiot. This guy had a knife and obviously intended to kill me. I can't believe he hurt Gina instead. And—" she raised her eyes to his, silently marveling at their grayish blue intensity "—I'd be putting you in danger if I stayed here. I don't want to be responsible for anyone else getting hurt."

Wesley easily stepped over the table and knelt in front of her. He took her hands in his and looked deep into her eyes. "I can take care of myself, Destiny. I can also take care of you."

"Which brings me to my next point. I don't understand why you're doing this. What's in it for you?"

Something flashed in his eyes before his expression closed and became unreadable. "Why are you so suspicious of my motives?"

"Because," she said as she gave her hands a fruitless tug, "people don't just help other people for no reason."

"You help Gina. You help your father."

"Because I know them and love them. That's two reasons."

"I know you," he said. "And I'd be happy to make love to you."

Destiny gave him a warning look. "How did you get through medical school when all your thoughts seem to emanate from below your belt?"

"A doctor has to have a full understanding of anatomy."

"I have no doubt that you excelled in your study of anatomy."

Wesley gave her a spine-melting smile. "I'd be happy to review yours."

"Pass, thanks," she told him, jerking her hands away. "Which is precisely why I shouldn't stay here. You can't talk to me without innuendo and double entendre."

"I can be good," he said, feigning innocence.

"I'm sure you have numerous testimonials to your credit from a few hundred of your most recent conquests."

"Now who's the one spouting innuendo?"

"Sorry. But you and I don't seem to be able to communicate on a very meaningful level."

"I thought we were communicating just fine last night."

Destiny groaned and got out of the chair, needing to distance herself from those bedroom eyes and that velvety voice. The man purred like a pro.

"You're making my argument for me," she said from a safe distance. "I don't want to spend my days being harassed by you. I'm not in your league, Wesley."

"My league?"

"You know," she insisted, twisting the end of her braid around her fingers. "You're obviously very much at home trading come-ons. And I didn't even go to college."

"They don't teach come-ons in college," Wesley remarked.

She let out an exasperated breath. "You know what I mean. We're from different worlds. We have nothing in common, and we have no business sharing the same address.''

"Why is it so hard for you to accept my help?"

"It has nothing to do with accepting help."

"You're kidding yourself," he said in that calm, analytical voice. "You're resisting my help because you can't stand the thought of someone calling the shots for you."

"What?" she fairly screamed. "That's crazy."

"Is it?" he asked, taking a few steps so that they stood toe-to-toe in the dining room. "I've watched you with Gina and David. Your sense of responsibility, while admirable, has put you in a position of being caretaker for the two of them. Then you have your father. He seems very able to pull your strings at will. You put up with it because you love him, but also because you'd have to answer to your mother if you didn't."

"Are you finished?"

"Not quite," he said, his voice rising slightly. "You go out of your way to avoid conflict. But this stalker isn't going to let you avoid him. He's already crossed into the final phase."

"What final phase?"

Wesley placed his hands firmly on her shoulders. "He falls in love with you. He feels rejected when you don't return the affection. The rejection manifests itself in the form of anger. When he can't deal with the anger, he acts out. He sends notes and gifts, little reminders of how much you've hurt him. He wants you to know that all of his bad feelings are your fault."

"That's crazy."

"I didn't say it was rational. I'm simply outlining the behavior."

"It isn't making me feel any better."

Wesley's expression softened, as did his grip. "When you didn't react to his notes, you changed from an obsession to an enemy."

"You are really scaring me," she admitted.

"Last night he proved that he won't give up until he's caused you as much pain as he thinks you've caused him."

"So what am I supposed to do?"

"Stay here. Let Dylan and me see what we can turn up."

"But I have to work."

"You can," he promised as his hand slid over her throat to cup her cheek. "You'll just have a shadow while you're doing it."

"But why you?"

Wesley didn't say anything, but his eyes told her volumes. She saw very clearly a private hurt that tugged at the corners of her heart.

"What sin are you atoning for?" she pressed.

"A very major one," he reluctantly admitted.

Chapter Ten

"I let someone down once. Someone I cared very deeply for."

Destiny saw the flicker of pain dull the brilliance of his eyes. That pain chipped into her resolve. "I'm sorry."

"It was a long time ago," he said after expelling a slow breath. Wesley's expression lightened after that, as the sexy half smile erased the haunting memory. "So be a sport and allow me to redeem myself. Okay?"

Common sense, reason and her intelligence all told her to say thanks, but no thanks. However, the word "sure" somehow spilled from her lips.

Wesley patted her knee and stood.

"But," she amended, "I want your word that you'll stop harassing me."

He feigned deep hurt. "Me?"

She gave him a sidelong glance. "I won't provide you with the opportunity for redemption if you won't give me your word that you'll stop hitting on me at every opportunity."

He pensively stroked the shadow of a beard along

his jawline. "I promise not to make you uncomfortable."

"That isn't what I said."

He stood in front of her, his hands braced on his hips, his legs shoulder width apart. The stance wasn't threatening so much as it was authoritative. "I can't promise you that I won't try, Destiny. I'm attracted to you. I think you're attracted to me."

"But we're adults. We don't have to act on our attractions."

"Maybe you don't," he reasoned. "But I believe you and I would be wonderful together."

A small sound of disbelief rumbled in her throat. "You don't know me. You can't possibly have a rational reason for reaching that conclusion."

"Maybe my attraction to you negates my reason."

WESLEY ARRIVED at The Rose Tattoo wearing deep worry lines at the corners of his eyes.

"What's wrong?" Susan asked when he met her on the stairs.

He smiled at the waitress. "Just mulling over a small problem."

Susan wrinkled her nose as she studied him. "I'm sensing more than just a small problem," she told him in that grave, intense voice that she adopted whenever she was about to pass along one of her psychic insights. "Your aura is bright red."

"My aura is just tired," he told her. "I had a rough night last night."

Susan's eyes grew wide. "Were you with her last night? I heard about the break-in on the radio. Did someone really try to kill Destiny?"

Wesley shrugged and nodded. "He made a gallant attempt."

"And you were there?" Susan pressed, clearly excited by his revelation. "What happened?"

For all her oddball propensities, Wesley liked Susan. He lifted one foot onto the next step and leaned against the wall. "Someone broke in and—"

"Was that other woman really stabbed? Was there really a shoot-out?"

"Calm yourself," he said as he placed a hand on her shoulder. "Gina was stabbed but she's going to be fine, and there was no shoot-out."

Susan appeared shocked. "I've never known anyone who's been stabbed."

His mouth pulled into a tight line. "Be thankful. It isn't a pretty sight."

"No wonder your aura is so screwed up," she said with conviction. "You need to meditate to adjust your karma after a terrible thing like that."

"I'll take that under advisement," he promised. "Is my mother in her office?"

Susan nodded. "Yep. Shelby's here with the terrible twosome."

He left Susan, refusing her offer to consult her tarot cards. He took the stairs two at a time, reaching the second floor in short order.

His mother's establishment was a converted Charleston Single House. The long, narrow building dated back to the romantic, prosperous days when Charleston was the hub of antebellum southern society. The rich paneling and ornate carvings had lasted more than a century. He ran his fingers along the smooth wood as he walked toward the familiar voices.

He found his mother seated behind her desk, applying a coat of bright orange polish to her nails. Chad Tanner was in one corner, sorting colored paper clips into piles. Shelby was at her desk with two-month-old Cassidy sleeping against her shoulder.

"Please tell me the reports I heard this morning weren't true," Rose said without preamble.

"She wasn't attacked, was she?" Shelby asked.

Wesley leaned against the credenza and raked his hands through his hair. "The story's been embellished, but the guy made his move last night."

Rose's green eyes narrowed, and Shelby's expression was one of uncomfortable recognition.

Shelby gently patted her infant daughter on the back. "How awful that Gina was hurt. Will she be all right?"

"They're going to keep her in the hospital a few days, but her wounds weren't life threatening."

"I'll bet she doesn't feel that way," Rose scoffed. "What about Destiny?"

"She's upset," Wesley answered. "She's at my place."

Rose's reaction to his statement was predictable. She got that conniving gleam in her eyes that he'd seen when she was orchestrating the courtship of his older brother, J.D.

"My building is safe."

"Is that the only reason?" Rose queried as one perfectly shaped brow lifted in the direction of her radically teased hair.

He had to smile at the hopeful expression.

"I didn't think she should be alone."

"You could have handed her off to that annoying manager of hers," Rose stated. "Or you could have brought her to me."

"Or me," Shelby added.

"I could have," he conceded, schooling himself so as not to get his mother's hopes up.

"She can have our sofa," Shelby suggested. "I'm sure Dylan wouldn't mind."

But I would, he thought as he fixed his attention on the little boy bending the paper clips into strange configurations. "She's fine where she is," he told them.

"What about her father?" Rose asked. "He wasn't hurt, was he?"

"No," he said. Wesley turned to Shelby and found her looking terribly frightened. "I guess this dredges up some pretty bad memories for you."

Her eyes went from him to Chad, then back again. "I'll never forget what it was like when he was missing. I won't forget the calls, that voice..."

Rose moved over and placed a comforting hand on Shelby's shoulder. Baby Cassidy sighed and wriggled, but she didn't awaken.

"Don't get lost in the past," Rose said to Shelby, though she was looking directly at him. "You learn from it and move on."

"I keep reminding myself that everything worked out in the end," Shelby lamented. "But sometimes I still hear that voice in my dreams. I remember how helpless I felt when Chad was gone."

"Bye-byes?" Chad asked, abandoning the pile of paper clips.

"Not yet," Shelby said to her son, ruffling his dark hair as she spoke. "We have to wait for Daddy."

"Daddy," Chad repeated. Then he poked the sleeping infant. "Baby."

"Cassidy," Shelby said slowly.

"Baby," Chad told her forcefully before he scurried back to his game.

"He's a real conversationalist," Shelby groaned.

"He does okay," Wesley told her.

"He's almost two years old and still not using sentences."

"He'll get there," Wesley assured her. "The Sesame Street police won't arrest you unless he enters first grade with a single-word vocabulary."

"Very funny," Shelby said. "Wait until you have kids. You worry about their development at every stage."

"His development is fine," Wesley reassured her. "Cut him some slack. In a few years you'll long for the days when he was quiet."

"What makes you such an expert?" Rose said with a snort. "I think you should keep your opinions to yourself until you have a few kids of your own."

"Don't hold your breath," Wesley said.

"That's right." Rose sighed theatrically. "You're never getting married."

He felt his annoyance level rising.

Rose continued, "You don't think you can balance a medical career and a family."

"Mother," he warned.

"Don't 'mother' me. I could understand your position if you were still planning a hectic life in the ER. But since you've made the switch to psychiatry, I don't see the problem."

"Drop it, please," Wesley warned.

"You'll regret this," Rose argued.

"Maybe," he said in hopes of getting her off the subject. "Right now I need to find Dylan. Know where he is?"

"He's working at home," Shelby answered. "He'll be there until around four. I brought the tag team here to give him some peace and quiet."

Wesley glanced at his watch. "Think he'll mind if I stop in unannounced?"

"Not at all. If you leave now, you two can have about an hour of peace before he collects us."

He tickled Chad on his way out, leaving the little boy rasping with laughter on the floor.

The midday sun beat down on him as he exited the restaurant. The air was thick with the fragrance of the flowers planted along the path that connected the bar to the club. He couldn't look at the dependency without thinking of his brother. Not that he dared ever admit it to anyone, but he would have liked to have his older brother around.

"What am I doing?" he asked as he slipped behind the wheel of his car. "I'm not equipped to protect a woman against a stalker."

He told Dylan exactly that when he arrived at the Tanner household. He'd found Dylan in the backyard, yelling at an unruly mixed breed.

"Come here, Foolish!"

The dog darted just out of Dylan's grip. Wesley swallowed his laughter each time the dog countered one of Dylan's attempts to catch him.

"Well-trained beast," Wesley observed.

Dylan gave him a warning look. "I hate that dog."

Foolish barked.

"I think he hates you, too."

"Then he can stay out here until Shelby gets back."

On that note, Dylan opened the gate and led Wesley in through the kitchen door. Foolish remained outside, his leash firmly clamped in his mouth.

The Tanners' home smelled of baby. Wesley took in the comfortable surroundings—the toys, the clutter—and wondered why he hadn't noticed those things on previous visits. It was as if he was seeing the simple domesticity for the first time. He chalked the observation up to serious sleep deprivation.

"I saw the report on the stabbing when I was at the office," Dylan said as he grabbed two cans of soda from the refrigerator.

Wesley turned one of the kitchen chairs backward and sat down with his elbows resting on the back edge. "It was pretty bad," he said as he flipped the metal tab on the can.

"Everyone okay other than the Alverez woman?"

"Destiny's spooked, but she'll manage. I'll make sure she's safe."

Dylan joined him at the table, eyeing him curiously.

"Don't you start on me, too."

"Meaning?" Dylan asked.

"My mother is already planning a wedding. It isn't like that."

"Is that why she's in residence at your place?"

Wesley questioned the other man with his eyes.

Dylan shrugged. "I called Greavy and he told me Destiny went home with you."

"It seemed like a good idea under the circumstances. I couldn't very well stick her in a hotel."

"You could have brought her here."

"Shelby said the same thing."

Dylan smiled. "I know, she called before you got here."

"Destiny is welcome to stay with me until they catch this creep."

Dylan took a swallow of his soda. "Creep? I thought you were convinced he was a delusional individual suffering from a personality break."

"I hate it when people quote me," he grumbled.

"Then don't emote," his friend suggested. "I may have something on that paper we found attached to the card."

Wesley experienced a surge of excitement. "Think you'll be able to track the guy?"

Dylan lifted his shoulders in a noncommittal shrug. "Depends. I sent the note and the paper over to the CPD."

"You're not going to take care of this yourself?"

"I kept a copy," Dylan assured him. "I've got one of our interns checking the logo fragment against the ads in the Yellow Pages."

"Why?"

"Because the card is probably from the florist's shop where the flowers were purchased."

"Won't CPD do the same thing?"

"Eventually," Dylan answered. "Right now their primary interest is the assault on Gina. Oh," Dylan said as he took another sip of his soda, "I heard you did a pretty fair job on her until the EMTs arrived."

"I didn't do much."

"That's not the way I heard it."

Wesley shifted restlessly in his chair. "It was no big deal."

"C'mon, Wes," Dylan prodded. "Why are you so uncomfortable with this? I bet it earned you a few brownie points with Destiny."

"We weren't keeping score at the time."

"You certainly are touchy about this."

"I'm just tired of people questioning my motives. The woman was hurt, so I helped. Destiny was in danger, so I gave her a safe place to stay."

"And all of your motives were pure?" Dylan asked.

Wesley lowered his eyes and felt a small smile tug at the corners of his mouth. "So, there are worse things than waking up with Destiny Talbott in your bed." Wesley didn't bother to mention that he had spent the night on the sofa.

"My last boyfriend was a real loser," she told the audience. "He was so stupid, he referred to second grade as his senior year." Destiny slipped the microphone into place and said, "Thank you all, you've been great."

She left the stage in a hurry, silently cursing under her breath.

"That was great," Wesley said.

"Hardly," she snapped as she dabbed her forehead with the towel she had grabbed off a stool in the hallway. "My timing was terrible."

"I thought you did fine," he said as he followed her into her dressing room.

"You're a doctor, not a comic," Destiny argued. Grabbing her robe off the back of the chair in front of her dressing table, she slipped behind the screen and peeled off her costume. "I blew the punch line on the trailer-park story. I didn't set up the joke about Congress. I didn't—"

"They laughed," Wesley broke in. "You entertained them. That's what they paid for."

She peeked around the edge of the barricade. "I was terrible," she assured him. "I haven't been that off in years."

"Don't sweat it," he cajoled. "You have five and a half more weeks to practice."

"Thanks," she grumbled as she belted her robe. "I've been getting worse," she called out. "Ever since Gina was stabbed, I've been off."

"You had a major life crisis."

"Don't analyze me," she implored. "Just let me rant and rave until I get it out of my system. That's what Gina always did."

"I think that's what's bothering you."

"Brilliant deduction," she said. "How am I supposed to feel? Gina still won't see me."

"Give her time, Destiny. She'll come around."

"I hope you're right," she told him as she moved to the dressing table. She looked up at his reflection in the mirror.

Wesley Porter's handsome features still had the ability to take her breath away. He looked particularly attractive this evening. His dark hair was combed neatly off his forehead. It curled slightly at the ends where it brushed the collar of his polo shirt. His eyes very nearly matched the blue shade of the shirt, though the eye color was far more intense. The way he looked at her from behind those glasses was something that unnerved Destiny. He had this uncanny ability to make her feel as if she was stark naked no matter what the situation.

"Stop doing that," she warned.

"Doing what?"

"Looking at me like that."

"Like what?" he asked, his voice seductive and innocent.

"Like you're taking my clothes off with your eyes."

"You don't have any clothes on," he countered as he moved to stand behind her.

"I do, too," she huffed, pinching the edges of her robe to her throat.

Wesley bent down, though their eyes remained locked in the mirror. He spoke with his breath tantalizing her earlobe. "But I live for the memory of you in that hot tub."

"You," she began as she reached back and gave him a small shove, "are a horrible man."

"I'm hurt," he said with a sigh.

"Not yet," she countered as she unscrewed the lid to her cleanser. "But I'd be happy to inflict a few well-placed wounds if you don't stop hitting on me. I thought we had a deal."

"I haven't hit on you at home."

Destiny glared at him for a second before beginning the process of removing her makeup. "You hit on me when we went back to the villa to get my things. You hit on me when I was having lunch with your mother. You hit on me when we went to the grocery store."

"My point exactly. I haven't violated our agreement. I haven't said one word at home."

"Then we need to amend our agreement."

"I'll amend our agreement if you'll admit that you like me."

"Not in your lifetime," she assured him.

"Is that any way to treat the man who has provided you with a roof over your head?"

"I can cover my own head," she said, struggling to keep from smiling in response to the teasing light in his eyes. "If you want loyalty and gratitude, I suggest you get a dog."

"It wouldn't be the same," he said as he took his finger and tapped the tip of her nose. "You're house-broken."

"Be still, my heart," she drawled. "You sure do know how to make a girl feel special."

Wesley pressed up behind her and placed his hands on her shoulders. Destiny watched him in the mirror; his smile was at strict odds with the determination she saw in his eyes. His fingers kneaded her tense muscles. She could feel the outline of his body where it pressed against hers.

"What are you doing?" she asked, hoping he hadn't heard the small catch in her voice.

"I'm trying to make you feel special," he murmured in that deep, sexy voice that caused a flutter in her stomach.

His thumbs made maddening circles against her spine as he slipped his hands beneath the collar of her robe. The sensation of his warm, slightly callused hands on her bare flesh caused her back to arch in response. Destiny drew her bottom lip between her teeth to keep from moaning as he explored the slope of her throat. The tips of his fingers found the sensitive spot just above her collarbone. Throughout his silent exploration, his eyes remained locked with hers in the mirror.

"You have incredibly soft skin," he whispered.

"I'm a girl."

"I noticed."

His fingers dipped lower, brushing the lacy edge of her bra. She sucked in her breath at the contact and dropped the jar of cleanser.

"Look what you made me do."

"It's nice to know you aren't as immune as you pretend," he said through a very satisfied grin.

"Help me clean this up," she said as she slipped from the chair and tried to salvage as much of the expensive botanical mixture as possible. "I can't believe this," she complained. "Do you have any idea how much this stuff costs?"

Dropping onto one knee, Wesley tended to the small pool with a fistful of tissues. "I'll replace it."

"You can't. It's mail order."

"So I'll order some."

"That won't do me much good if I run out."

"Are you mad because you dropped this, or because I touched you?"

"Just clean, Wesley," she instructed.

He did as she asked, but the infuriating man actually whistled while he was at it. His cheerful attitude and relaxed movements did little to improve her mood. The man was positively incorrigible. It took all her self-control to keep from kicking him while he was down.

"All done." Wesley beamed as he wiped away the last smear of white cream. "You didn't answer my question."

"And I'm not going to," she assured him as she finished removing the last of her stage makeup.

"If you won't talk, I'll have to test my theory in my own way."

"What are you talking about?"

"A scientific approach."

Wesley moved in behind her again, taking a lock of her hair between his fingers. The smoldering look in his eyes communicated more than she was ready to hear.

"You aren't being scientific, you're being pushy."

"Pushy, huh?" he repeated, apparently mulling it over in his mind. "I like to think of myself as persistent, not pushy."

"Semantics."

"Just for the sake of science," he began as he gathered her hair in a fist and lifted it off her neck, "why don't I nuzzle your neck for a little while? Just until you scream and claw my clothes off."

"That's it," Destiny said as she jumped off the chair and went to the door. She pulled it open. "You can wait outside."

She expected him to take her rejection in stride. It wasn't as if it was the first time she'd tossed him out of her dressing room. It was the third, to be precise. But his reaction this time was very different. Wesley was looking out the door when she saw his face grow hard. The light in his eyes vanished and his lips were pulled into a taut, angry line.

Following his line of sight, Destiny looked down. Then she saw it.

Chapter Eleven

"Christ," Wesley muttered as he moved past her and knelt in front of the grotesquely painted doll.

She watched in silent horror as he flicked his fingernail against the handle of the knife protruding from the doll's chest. The doll was almost identical to the first one—thick blond curls glued to the head, the lips stained with a bright red paint, even the eyes colored a vivid violet.

"It looks so much like me," Destiny whispered.

Wesley rose, pulled her into his arms and began gently stroking her back. She swallowed deep breaths of his cologne, trying to concentrate on anything but the terror churning in her stomach. She was determined not to fall apart. Still, seeing the knife sticking out of the doll brought back a flood of memories.

"We should call the cops."

"Okay." She flattened her palms against his solid chest. "He was right outside the door."

"I know," Wesley said, his voice hard and steely. "Let's hope someone saw him."

"What am I going to do?" she asked, squeezing her eyes shut as he soothingly stroked her hair.

"We're going to find this guy."

While she appreciated the sentiment, Destiny didn't share Wesley's conviction. They had only her creepy fan, and Destiny just couldn't bring herself to believe he was her stalker.

With Wesley standing guard at the door, Destiny changed into a pair of jeans and a blouse. She left her hair loose and stepped into her well-worn espadrilles. The rumble of approaching footsteps sent her flying into Wesley's arms.

"It's Greavy," Wesley told her as he draped his arm across her shoulders.

Destiny spent the next hour being questioned by the puzzled police officer, who promised to interview her obsessive fan at the first opportunity. Wesley remained at her side but said nothing. Her only insight into his thoughts was his eyes. They were like blue ice, hard and cold. The controlled anger she saw sent a chill down her spine. For all his calm and politeness, Destiny decided, the man had a dangerous streak.

"I'll take you home now," he said once Greavy and his men had carted off the doll.

"I'm afraid to go outside," she admitted when he reached for her hand.

Lacing her fingers with his, Wesley said, "I'm not going to let anything happen to you."

"You may not have the last word on that subject."

"I always get the last word on really important stuff," Wesley promised.

The late-night air was refreshingly cool. Crickets serenaded the low-hung moon as she and Wesley went to his car. Destiny was wary of every shadow, every leaf, every noise. By the time she locked herself into the car, her palms were sweaty and her heart was pounding against her rib cage. *I'm having a heart at-*

tack, she told herself. That was the only plausible explanation for the pressure building in her chest.

She began to breathe short, raspy breaths that didn't seem to satisfy her need for air.

"You're hyperventilating," Wesley said as he turned in his seat and cupped her face in his hands. Destiny grabbed at his wrists. "Look at me," he instructed.

She stared into the blue depths of his eyes, wondering at the frightening feelings.

"It's okay," he said softly. "Concentrate on taking deep, long breaths. That's it, keep looking at me."

The incessant pounding of her heartbeat in her ears began to fade, and she no longer felt as if her chest would explode.

"Better?" Wesley asked as he wiped at her cheeks with the pads of his thumbs.

Destiny felt the dampness and only then realized that tears had spilled from her eyes. "I thought I was going to die," she admitted in a small voice.

Wesley offered her a lopsided smile. "You're not allowed to die in my presence. I'd probably lose my doctor status if my lady died in my car."

My lady? she repeated in her brain. Figure of speech, she concluded. "I'm sorry, I don't know what happened to me."

Wesley continued to stroke her cheek. "Panic attack," he explained. "Nothing permanent."

"Easy for you to say," she countered with a forced smile. "You weren't the one whose heart was dancing a jig like some disgusting special effect in a teen slash-and-splatter flick."

His smile reached his eyes. "I don't think I've ever heard it described quite like that."

The tension in her took on a new character. What had been frightening evolved into a purely feminine awareness. Destiny quietly searched his face, sensing he somehow understood the change.

He saw the change in her. It was subtle, but he instinctively knew it when he saw it. He threw the car in gear and drove quickly back to the condo.

Days and nights of wanting her fortified him as he unlocked the door. Flipping on the light, Wesley looked down at her mouth, which was lifted into a gentle curve of a smile. The sight eased the nervous uncertainty that knotted his gut.

She stood with her back against the wall, her eyes searching his face. He wanted to grab her and run into the bedroom, but knew better. The last thing he wanted to do was scare her.

He placed his palms on the cool surface of the wall on either side of her head. He sensed that the unease in her was more than just sexual, and it scared him. For the first time in his adult life, Wesley wasn't getting a clear signal. He sighed and battled the strong urge to press his body into hers, let her feel the extent of his need for her.

"I can make you forget all about dolls, guns, knives and flowers," he told her huskily. "But I want it to be your decision." He removed his glasses and placed them on the hall table.

"That's very gallant of you," she said in a breathy, almost strangled voice.

"I'm not trying to be gallant," he insisted. "I'm having a hard time getting a fix on this."

"A fix?"

Wesley rested his forehead on hers, savoring the feminine scent of her smooth skin. "I don't want to push you, but I don't think I can keep my hands off you any longer."

"You've never kept your hands off me," she teased.

He stared as her tongue darted out to moisten her bottom lip. Her mouth glistened in the pale glow of the room's soft light.

"Please, Destiny. Tell me what you want. Quickly."

"I'm not sure," she said as her hands flattened against his chest.

Wesley felt the slight tremor in her hands. "Are you afraid?"

"Not afraid," she answered quickly. "Uncertain."

He smiled. "I think I can help you make up your mind."

The mere hint of a smile was enough encouragement. Wesley wrapped her in his arms and held her for a second as he reined in his own fierce desire. Entwining his fingers in her silken hair, he relished the feel of her soft body against his. He was vividly aware of the swell of her breasts and the taut flatness of her stomach. He could also feel his body's immediate response.

Her hands skimmed the tight muscles of his back, her fingers exploring the contour of his spine. But she made no move to pull him to her—or to push him away.

He was very nearly going out of his mind, his need was so great. His self-control was dwindling, being overcome by his primitive desire to have her begging and pleading for his touch. He didn't want her simply to enjoy. He wanted her totally wild, as desperate to consummate the relationship as he was.

With that goal in mind, he lowered his mouth and began teasing the seam of her lips with his tongue.

Leisurely he tasted her, savoring the heat, reining in his own passions in order to inspire hers. He kissed her softly, almost tentatively, angling her face beneath him by gently tugging the hair tangled in his hands. He felt her nails dig into the planes of his back as he slipped his tongue into the warm recesses of her mouth.

Deepening the kiss, Wesley dropped one hand to her waist and urged her against him. She complied willingly, even enthusiastically. He kissed her as if she were the only woman on earth. His brain scrambled in order to make sense of his conflicting emotions. Why did this feel so different? So right? It was passionate yet comfortable. Having Destiny in his arms felt as natural as taking his next breath.

"You taste like mint," he said against her mouth just before he lifted her off the ground.

"Where are you taking me?"

"The bedroom," he answered as he cradled her against him.

It wasn't until he reached the bedroom that he realized he'd been holding his breath, afraid she'd call a halt to things. Carefully he placed her in the center of the bed, then slid up beside her. Placing his leg over hers, Wesley searched her upturned face.

"This is much better," he murmured as he buried his face against her throat. Her skin tasted fresh and clean. No cologne or perfume, just Destiny. It was a heady scent.

She could hardly breathe. He was exciting, strong and solid. The weight of his leg fell across her abdomen, pressing against the core of her desire. It was becoming more and more impossible to keep her passion in check.

She sighed and lifted her lashes when his mouth trailed a fiery path to her lips. He kissed her again as he shifted in order to work his leg between hers. The intimacy of the action lanced through her, forcing her to arch against him as her primal instincts responded.

"Wesley," she whispered against his mouth, knowing full well it was now or never.

He made a strangled, guttural sound that tugged at her resolve. "Don't," he pleaded as he lifted his head.

The raw sensuality in his voice was almost as erotic as the feel of his hand slinking up her rib cage.

His eyes locked with hers. "Don't stop me now. It will be good," he said as his mouth dipped to her throat. "So good."

"I know," she admitted as she clamped her eyes closed. "That's what I'm afraid of."

He caught her face between his hands. She noted a slight tremor in his square-tipped fingers. "You're driving me crazy, Destiny. Do you have any idea how much I want you?"

"I think I have an idea," she teased, arching her body against the unmistakable evidence of his desire.

A deep, rich moan rumbled in the back of his throat. Destiny felt very powerful at that instant. It had a heady effect on her. She slipped her arms around his neck and drew him down to her. Opening her mouth eagerly beneath his, she banished all doubt from her brain. This felt too right to be wrong.

"Tell me you want me," he instructed in a nearly desperate whisper. "I need to hear the words."

"I want you."

"Finally." He sighed as he moved to cover her body with his.

Wesley wasn't sure what was driving him. He really

didn't care. He was too lost in the thrill of unbuttoning her blouse. Much to his pleasure, Destiny was doing some exploring of her own. She had opened his shirt, and her fingers splayed across his chest.

She stroked upward, flattening her palms against his nipples. "You feel strong," she breathed admiringly.

Wesley thought he'd burst with male pride. It was the first time she'd offered a compliment, and it did amazing things to his ego.

"You feel soft," he murmured as he spread open her shirt.

Wesley propped himself up by his elbow and peered down as his fingers made easy work of the front clasp to her lacy brassiere. Her skin was flawlessly smooth and pleasantly flushed. He covered one of her breasts with his hand, rolling the taut nipple beneath his palm. She sucked in a quivering breath.

He could feel her heart beating against his hand, feel the urgency of her response. He molded her in his hand, manipulating the sensitive bud between his thumb and forefinger. Destiny made a half-strangled sound and his hand stilled.

"Did I hurt you?" he asked.

"Not exactly," she told him with a wry smile. "I've never been touched quite like that."

"Really?"

"You're watching," she explained.

"I am, aren't I?" Wesley grinned down at her. "Does that bother you?"

"A little," she admitted as her lashes fluttered over her fiery violet eyes.

"But you're beautiful," he insisted as he traced her puckered, mauve skin with the tip of his finger. "You have nothing to be embarrassed about. Trust me."

He heard her sharp intake of breath as his mouth closed on her body. She went rigid beneath him, then arched her back as her hands gripped the back of his head.

"You're making me crazy," she told him.

"Good." Wesley made quick work of dispensing with their clothes. He took his time exploring every cell of her body. She was the most exquisite creature he'd ever encountered. Her body was flawless, her reactions genuine. When he finally buried himself inside her in one heartfelt thrust, Wesley was half out of his mind with need. She matched him move for move. It was so perfect, so right—as if the whole thing had been choreographed ahead of time. He tried to make it last, wanted it to go on forever, but even he reached the breaking point. He groaned as the need spilled from his body in an incredible, mind-shattering release.

Much later she lay huddled in the crook of his arm, her eyes wide and fixed on the watercolor hanging above the desk. Judging from the steady rise and fall of his chest and the even rhythm of his breathing, Wesley had finally fallen asleep.

Destiny carefully and silently slipped from the bed, grabbing her clothing from the mingled pile on the floor. Her cheeks burned hotly as she tiptoed out into the living room.

"I'm an idiot," she groaned as she pulled on her slacks. "I screwed up big time."

She felt a little better with her clothes on, but not much. Part of her wanted to go to the window, throw it open and tell the world that she'd just had the most incredible, toe-curling experience of her life. Another part of her simply wanted to jump from that window and fall slowly to a painful death.

She glared at her reflection in the chrome finish of the coffee machine. "You were a fool to do something that stupid," she berated in a harsh whisper. "You can die, you can get pregnant, you can—"

"No, you can't," Wesley cut in.

Destiny spun on the ball of her foot and found him lounging in the doorway, shirtless, disheveled and looking sexy as hell. It did little for her very bad mood.

"Well," Wesley amended with a slight incline of his dark head, "I suppose you could be pregnant."

She groaned. "Thanks."

"Why are you mad at me? You could have suggested I—"

"You're a doctor, for God's sake. You're supposed to know better."

Wesley scowled darkly. "Forgive me. I was a little caught up in the moment. Just as you were, as I recall."

She felt her cheeks grow even hotter. "It was a stupid and potentially fatal mistake."

He took two steps into the room, until he loomed above her looking angry and dangerous. "You needn't worry about diseases."

"Gee, thanks," she retorted sarcastically.

"That's not what's really bothering you, is it?"

Destiny met his eyes. "Heavens, no. I'm pleased as punch that I acted like some irresponsible wad of hormones."

"Wad of hormones?" he repeated with a throaty chuckle.

"It isn't funny!"

"No," he agreed. "But it isn't the end of the world, either."

"I suppose that depends on your perspective," she grumbled. "You aren't the one whose career would go down the drain in the event of unforeseen complications."

"Interesting euphemism for unplanned pregnancy."

Destiny let out a loud breath. "Leave me alone, Wesley. I don't want—"

"I think that's the real problem. You don't know what you want." He moved and gripped her shoulders, waiting until she raised her eyes to his. "You're not afraid of being pregnant. You're too adept at handling responsibility."

"Maybe I'm tired of responsibility," she suggested quietly.

He shook his head. "I think you're more afraid of your own response. I think it scared the hell out of you to lose control like you did."

"I think you have an ego the size of a small country."

"If the only problem is my ego, why are we standing in the middle of my kitchen at six in the morning?"

"So go to bed," she suggested with a saccharine smile.

"Come with me," he said, his voice deep, sultry and quite capable of penetrating the protective shell she was attempting to build.

"I need space," she told him, lowering her eyes to study the grout lines in the ceramic tile floor.

"I don't think it would be a smart idea to leave you out here just now."

"Why?"

"I can't begin to imagine the crazy things you'll—"

The ringing of the phone jarred them both. Destiny rubbed her arms as Wesley ripped the instrument from the wall.

"Porter."

She saw his expression darken just before he thrust the receiver in her direction.

"Hello?"

"It's me, David."

"Do you know what time it is?"

"Should I jump to the obvious conclusions?" David sneered.

"About what?"

"If he handed you the phone, I assume that means you were within arm's reach."

"We're standing in his kitchen," she informed him in clipped tones.

"Is something wrong?"

"Lots of things," she hedged. "I got another doll."

"When? Where?" David demanded before he let out a string of colorful expletives.

She filled him in on all the pertinent details.

David was quiet for a minute before he said, "I'm afraid I have some news that isn't going to make you feel any better."

"Is it my father?"

"Yep."

She let out a breath and closed her eyes briefly, praying for strength. "What jail is he in?"

"That's just it," David began. "I can't find him."

"You lost my father?" Destiny wailed. "How could you do that?"

"He left a note."

"Great," she snapped. "What else?"

"He said he was going to lie low until your stalker is caught."

That's my dad, she thought miserably. "What else?"

David cleared his throat before saying, "Walter's on his way. He isn't happy."

All her dreams, everything she'd worked for, seemed to be teetering on the brink of collapse.

"There's more," David admitted. "It's about Gina."

"Is she all right? Will she see me?" Destiny asked hurriedly.

"She's gone, too."

Chapter Twelve

"She's what?"

"Gone," David repeated. "They released her from the hospital last night."

"Where did she go?"

"I don't have a clue. She didn't say anything to me when I saw her at dinner."

Wesley issued a silent question with his eyes. Destiny shrugged her confusion. "You had dinner with her? How was she?"

"Distant. Pretty much the same."

She felt her spirits plummet. "I thought she'd come around." She nervously twisted her hair around her fingers. "I can't stand knowing she hates me."

"I don't think she hates you," David said with uncharacteristic kindness. "I'm sure once she realizes that she isn't permanently injured, she'll forgive and forget."

"I hope you're right." Destiny sighed. "Please keep looking for her."

"I'll do my best." There was a pointed silence before David asked, "Do you know what you're doing, honey? Porter isn't your usual—"

"Thanks for caring," she interrupted. "Did my father say where he was going?"

"There was nothing on the screen."

"The screen?" she asked, her eyebrows wrinkling.

"On my laptop. He typed his farewell."

Destiny shook her head, trying to clear away the dull yet insistent warning sounding in her mind. "My dad isn't computer literate," she told him. "At least, he wasn't a few months ago when I paid some typing service to transcribe his notes from his latest angst manuscript."

"It isn't a very complicated system. And knowing your dad, he probably just hit you up for the typing because he was too lazy to do it himself."

She could hardly argue with that. Her father had a long history of taking the easiest path between points. "Keep me posted."

"Keep *me* posted," David countered, censure dripped from every syllable. "I'm meeting Walter near his hotel for lunch. He wants you there, too. One-fifteen at Bocci on Church Street. Think you can find it?"

"I'll be there."

"Leave the boyfriend at home."

When the line went dead, she handed the phone to Wesley, replaying the conversation in her head.

"Trouble?"

"Gina and my father have disappeared."

"Disappeared?"

"Gina was discharged, and my father sneaked out of town and left a message on David's computer."

"Is that normal?"

She shrugged slightly. "He has a talent for disappearing whenever things get tough. I'm just a little surprised that he used David's laptop."

Wesley stroked his chin and his eyes narrowed contemplatively. "How surprised?"

"I've never known my father to go within ten feet of anything electronic. I don't think he can use a remote control, let alone a high-tech toy like a computer."

He mulled over her statement for a moment before grabbing the phone and pressing the keypad in determined, rapid motions.

Destiny wandered into the living room, needing space. She was bone tired, very confused and very, very afraid. Dread settled over her as she watched the sun peek over the horizon. The mere thought that she might not see Gina again was devastating. And her father's sudden disappearance was another potential disaster. Her mother would be quite distressed to hear that Carl Talbott was unaccounted for.

"Gina paid her bill in full before she was released."

"I gave them my card," Destiny reminded him. "I also told David to—"

"She paid cash," he interjected.

"Cash?" Destiny turned and looked into his eyes. "She doesn't have that kind of cash."

"Are you sure?"

"I had to give her an advance on her salary three weeks ago for her car insurance. Gina never had more than a few hundred dollars in the bank."

"I don't like this," Wesley murmured, crossing his forearms in front of his chest.

The action drew her eyes to the mat of thick, curly dark hair covering the sculpted, taut muscles. A shiver played along her spine as her mind produced vivid memories of what it felt like to press her face against that chest. The slight tickle from the hair when he moved...

"You listening?"

"I'm sorry." She coaxed the words from her suddenly dry throat. "What did you say?"

"I asked about Gina's habits. Where would she go?"

"Not back to the villa," Destiny told him with a humorless laugh. "Gina isn't big on returning to the scene of the crime. When we're home, she drives three miles out of her way just to avoid the road where she had the accident."

"Does she have any friends here? Anyone who would help her out?"

"No one," Destiny assured him. "Gina doesn't exactly cultivate friendships. She isn't much of a people person."

"Unlike you," he said softly as he came up in front of her.

Destiny lowered her eyes and tried not to fixate on the fact that the top button of his jeans lay open.

"I wouldn't get very far in this business if I adopted Gina's aloof air."

His finger hooked beneath her chin, forcing her to lift her head and meet his searching gaze. Destiny could easily lose herself in the shimmering blue depths of his eyes.

"What are you thinking?"

"Nothing."

He shook his head and gave her a sad, lopsided grin. "You don't lie very well. I can see you're still beating yourself up because we went to bed together."

Went to bed together. That sort of summed it up, she thought as she blinked back the threat of tears. "I guess I'm not particularly adept at casual affairs," she admitted as she slipped a bright smile into place. "I'll get over it. I *am* very adept at moving forward."

"You make it sound like this was a fluke."

"It was."

"Not from where I'm standing. Do you really think we'll be able to keep our hands off one another after what happened last night?"

Destiny gaped at him. "I think," she began, pausing for effect, "you have a colossal ego and some very serious delusions. I don't make a habit of repeating stupid mistakes."

"If you keep referring to me as a mistake, I might just get a complex."

"I doubt it," she said with a chuckle as she stepped away from him. "You are much too self-confident to let a little thing like rejection get you down."

"Where are you going?"

Destiny stopped just outside the bedroom door, but she didn't turn to face him. "I'm going to try to get a few hours of sleep before I have to meet Walter. Good night."

She closed the door and leaned against it. "You're between a rock and a hard place," she whispered.

SHE EMERGED from the bedroom several hours later. No better rested, but with a plan. She found Wesley hunched over the dining room table, fully immersed in an open textbook. He didn't seem to notice her presence, which gave her an opportunity to study his handsome profile.

Seeing him sitting there, his head resting against his palm, rattled her. He exuded a lazy, relaxed confidence that only made her feel more like an emotional house of cards. Moistening one finger with his tongue, Wesley turned the page. She noticed everything—the way his broad shoulders were slightly rounded as he pored over the material; his habit of rubbing his fingernail across the pad of his thumb as he concentrated. But most of all, she was aware of the unmistakable fact that he could tune her out with apparent ease.

"Obviously, I read more into last night than you did," she said under her breath.

"What?" he asked, lifting his head and looking in her direction.

"I asked if you'd been reading all this time?"

Flexing the muscles of his arms and shoulders, Wesley sighed and leaned back in the chair. "It feels that way. Did you get some sleep?"

"Not really." She could have sworn she saw a flash of satisfaction in his eyes. "Look," she began nervously, "I think it would be best if I left. I'll make arrangements to stay at a hotel until—"

"The guy kills you?" he interjected, his jaw rigid, his mouth a tight, angry line.

"I prefer to believe he'll be caught before that happens."

"Don't hold your breath," Wesley muttered as he pulled off his glasses and tossed them on top of the open book. "You couldn't walk from the club to the car without falling to pieces. How do you think you'll be able to handle living alone?"

"I've lived alone for a long time," she said. "I'll just have to be careful."

"Part of being careful is not being stupid."

Her nervousness was washed away by a sudden wave of hostility. "I am not stupid."

"You're running out of here because you can't deal with what happened between us."

"I'm not running."

"Really," he challenged as he pushed away from the table. "Five bucks says you have your suitcases packed and waiting by the door."

Destiny felt her cheeks color. "So?"

"So that's running away."

"No. It's a simple matter of self-preservation."

Wesley cocked his head to one side and studied her quietly. "Does that mean you don't trust yourself around me?"

"It means," she began tightly, "that now is not a good time for me to be playing in the fast lane. Especially when I'm way out of my league."

"Is that a compliment?" he asked, laughter dancing in the clear blue of his eyes.

"It's an observation," she said with a sigh. "Look, Wesley, last night was a huge mistake."

"Depends on your perspective," he said.

Ignoring his barb, she continued. "I can't possibly get involved with you right now. I've got a lunatic dogging my every move. My best friend isn't speaking to me, and Walter has come breezing into town, quite possibly to pull his funding."

"Funding for what?"

"He's producing the sitcom I mentioned. Without his backing, I don't have a snowball's chance."

He nodded pensively. "I don't see where our sleeping together has anything to do with your career aspirations."

Her eyes grew wide and she felt her mouth drop open as she stared at him. "I don't have casual affairs."

"Don't look now, but you're having one."

Her fists balled at her sides as frustration tensed every muscle in her body. "We aren't having an affair. We made a mistake, and the only way to keep from repeating it is for me to make alternative living arrangements."

He shrugged. "Not if I promise to keep my hands to myself."

"You can't."

"Now who's the one with the ego?" he drawled.

Closing her eyes, Destiny began silently counting to ten, then twenty. "I didn't mean it like that. I was referring to your penchant for hitting on me."

"No hitting," he returned easily. "Scout's honor."

"Are you trying to tell me you were a Boy Scout?"

"Of course I was. I used my first aid training in the ER."

"When were you in the ER?" she asked.

His expression clouded, effectively shutting out her only entry into his feelings.

"A lifetime ago."

The evasive, ominous tone of his voice piqued her interest. "As part of your medical training?"

"In a manner of speaking." He reached behind him to retrieve his glasses. Wesley made a production out of cleaning them on the tail of his well-worn denim shirt before slipping them into place on the bridge of his nose.

It was obvious that he wasn't going to elaborate. His secrecy only served to remind her that she didn't know much about him. She'd slept with him, but didn't really know anything about him.

"I have to meet Walter and David for lunch. I'll make arrangements with a hotel and move my things before I go to The Rose Tattoo tonight."

"What about your fan? You'll be an easy target in some hotel. And—" he paused as he leaned against the chair back "—have you thought about the fact that you'd be putting an innocent person in potential danger? What if the guy comes after you and repeats his last mistake? How will you feel if he stabs some maid?"

"You aren't helping," she grumbled.

"And, since you made the early news as well as page two of the paper, you'll hardly be able to lie low."

"What about you?" she argued. "According to your logic, you're risking your life by allowing me to stay here."

He shrugged. "It's my life."

"And your penance?"

Wesley was saved from answering by the interruption of the telephone. Destiny caught the scent of soap clinging to his impressive body as he brushed past her to grab the extension on the end table.

"Where are you?" she heard him ask in an excited voice. Cupping his hand over the mouthpiece, Wesley said, "It's Gina."

Snatching the phone out of his hand, Destiny urgently asked, "Where are you?"

"Listen," Gina began in a soft, frightened voice. "I've got to meet you, but you have to promise not to tell a soul that I've contacted you."

"Gina," Destiny wailed. "What are you talking about? And why are you whispering?"

"I want your word."

The stress in Gina's voice caused alarms to ring in her head. Destiny was at a loss to understand this strange behavior. "Have you been drinking?"

"Destiny." Gina said her name like a plea. "I want your word that you won't tell anyone I've contacted you."

"You aren't making sense."

"I will, as soon as I've had a chance to explain everything to you."

"What is it?" Destiny persisted, feeling Wesley's fingers at the small of her back. So much for keeping his hands to himself, she thought.

"I don't want to tell you over the phone. Have Carl bring you to—"

"My father took off." There was a long silence on the other end. "Are you still there?"

"When did he leave?"

"I don't know, exactly" she said. "Sometime during the night."

"Oh, my God," Gina cried. "Did David see him leave?"

"Nope. Apparently he sneaked out, but he left a note."

"Good."

Destiny felt the first stirrings of panic as she gripped the phone tightly in both hands. "Not so good," she amended. "The note was typed on David's laptop."

"By Carl?"

"I know," she agreed. "Strange, isn't it?"

"I can't believe this has gotten so out of hand."

"What has?"

"I'll tell you all about it. Can you meet me at Waterfront Park in an hour?"

"I have to meet Walter and David for lunch." Again the silence. "Gina? Are you there?"

"Don't go to lunch," Gina said. "Meet me instead. I'll explain everything."

"Not meet Walter?" she cried. "Have you forgotten that we need Walter?"

"It isn't safe," Gina said ominously. "You have to trust me on this."

"I do trust you," Destiny assured her, looking to Wesley for some assistance. "Are you taking anything?" she asked, hoping some sort of medication might account for Gina's paranoid behavior.

"I have to go," Gina told her. "Please say you'll meet me in the park."

"I will," Destiny assured her. "Let's say three o'clock."

"Please, Destiny," Gina pleaded. "Don't go to that lunch. I know I'm not making sense, but—"

"No," she interrupted, "you're not. Give me some valid reason for standing David and Walter up, and you know I'll consider it."

"It's more complicated than that," Gina groaned. "I can't explain it to you over the phone."

"Then I'll see you at three."

"At least take Wesley with you," Gina implored.

"I can't. David was very specific about that."

"I'm sure he was, but—"

There was a loud roar, followed by a loud click. "Gina?" she called. "Gina?" She met Wesley's questioning eyes and said, "She hung up."

"What was that all about?"

Destiny shrugged. "I haven't got a clue. She was very secretive. But she insisted I cancel my lunch and meet her at someplace called Waterfront Park." His hand fell away from her, leaving a void. "She sounded really strange."

"How so?"

"Agitated." She placed the receiver back on the cradle. "I know she and David have been having their professional differences."

"And you think that's why she didn't want you to keep your appointment?"

"It's the only thing that makes sense."

A CAB DROPPED HER at the restaurant, which was tucked into a stone alleyway in the historic section of the city. Destiny walked through the throng of tourists with her head hung low. She replayed her conversation with Gina over and over in her mind. Gina obviously wanted to confront her about something, but what?

Destiny scanned the restaurant and spotted David and Walter seated at a corner table, their heads bowed in hushed conversation. David looked tense and uneasy.

Walter seemed outwardly cool, thanks in large measure to his distinguished appearance. The shock of snow white hair, neatly styled, gave him the wealthy, cultured look of a man enjoying his success. The conservative, tailored suit and Italian leather shoes testified to his status. But it was more than just his physical appearance. Years of training in the courtroom had perfected his voice, hand gestures and body language. Walter Sommerfield had become a man who exuded control. Something Wesley Porter probably did from the moment of his birth.

"Stop thinking about him," she grumbled as she donned a smile and wove through the tables.

Both men rose as she reached the table.

"Destiny, my dear. You're looking lovely," Walter greeted, placing a kiss on her cheek. "I took the liberty of ordering for you. I hope you don't mind."

She did. "Of course not," she said. "Hi, David."

He smiled nervously before sitting and taking a long swallow from his wineglass.

"I'm very concerned about what's been happening. I should have been kept abreast of these developments," Walter announced when he was seated.

She patted the back of Walter's hand. The skin was soft and his evenly trimmed fingernails shone, probably a result of a recent professional buffing. "It's hard to believe someone doesn't like me, huh?"

One white brow arched high upon his forehead. "I don't believe this is a humorous matter."

Destiny felt her smile slip a notch. "Sorry."

Walter reached over and produced a folded newspaper. With a snap of his wrist he placed the paper in front of her. "This sort of publicity seriously jeopardizes your future."

Her publicity photo smiled up at her from the paper. The caption read Unfunny Business. Destiny cringed. "Not a very flattering article. They don't even mention my show times."

"Destiny," David groaned.

"You're the one who's always telling me any publicity is good."

David's jaw snapped shut and he shook his head.

"I'm concerned about your personal safety," Walter began. "I think it would be appropriate to cancel your current engagement. I can arrange for you to spend some time at my summer home in Connecticut."

"That isn't necessary," Destiny said, offering him a warm smile. "The police will find the guy and that will be the end of it."

"She's right," David offered. "And there's no guarantee she'll be any safer in Connecticut."

"That's a comforting thought," she murmured as she raised the water glass to her lips.

"But what about the injury to Miss Alverez?" Walter reasoned. "We can't place people in danger without running the risk of litigation."

"Gina won't sue me," Destiny assured him. "She didn't sue you," she reminded Walter gently. "And we're friends. Almost like sisters."

"Don't bet on it," she heard David whisper.

Walter's eyes flickered between Destiny and David. They were spun together in a web of tension, and she wondered how she could possibly choke down the chicken dish being placed before her.

"I spoke to Gina an hour ago," she informed David, pleased when she saw the flash of surprise in his eyes. "In fact, I'm meeting her later this afternoon."

"Did Miss Alverez give you any explanation for her behavior?" Walter asked.

"No," she admitted. "But we'll work things out. She was hurt because of me."

"Perhaps," Walter commented.

"C'mon, Destiny," David said. "You can't feel responsible for what happened to Gina. Especially not after what I learned this morning."

She didn't want to ask, but she knew she had no alternative. "What did you learn?"

David leaned forward and steepled his fingers as he rested his hands in front of him on the table. Walter took a fortifying sip of his chardonnay. The tension stretched as she waited for David to deliver his little bomb.

"I was going over the accounts," he began.

Destiny raised her hands, palms out. "If you're going to try and tell me Gina was skimming money, I don't want to hear it. I won't allow you to accuse Gina when she isn't around to defend herself."

"It isn't about money," David told her. "It's a little more serious than that."

"What?" she asked with nervous giggle. "I suppose you're going to tell me that Gina is the stalker and she somehow managed to stab herself."

Walter and David exchanged glances.

"Guys," Destiny prodded. "You can't be serious. Gina couldn't have stabbed herself—that would be crazy!"

Destiny's raised voice caught the attention of several other patrons. Feeling the warmth of a blush on her cheeks, she leaned forward and confronted David with a stern look. "You cannot possibly say anything that would convince me Gina has anything to do with this mess."

David looked at Walter, who nodded once. Her manager then reached under the table and produced a folder. Flipping it open, he removed several pieces of paper and tossed them in the center of the table.

Her eyes scanned the documents. It wasn't possible. Destiny took the top photocopy between her thumb and forefinger, plucking it like a tuft of lint.

"What is this supposed to prove?" she challenged, unwilling to accept the proffer.

"I believe it speaks for itself," Walter said with a sigh. "I also think we should take immediate legal action to ensure your safety on the off chance that Miss Alverez isn't working alone."

"This doesn't prove anything. For all we know, Gina might have a good explanation for this. Maybe she has a friend in a hospital," Destiny argued.

David snorted. "And maybe it's just a coincidence that she's been ordering gardenias the day before you receive them?"

Chapter Thirteen

She had the folder of incriminating photocopies tucked under her arm when the cab pulled up to the security gate at Wesley's building. She felt drained and exhausted. She didn't want to believe Gina was behind any of this.

"Good afternoon, Miss Talbott," the guard greeted before he pressed the button that opened the ornate gate leading to the parking lot.

Destiny smiled, though she knew the gesture failed to reach her eyes; nor did the smile she offered Wesley when he opened the door.

"Something happen?" he asked.

"Tough day at the office," she answered as she fell onto the sofa. "Has Gina called?"

"Sorry," he said as he sat next to her. "No word."

Destiny fixed her eyes on the worn weave of his jeans. "She didn't show at the park."

"What's with the folder?"

"David and Walter served me crow for lunch."

"Care to translate that for me?" he asked.

She opened the folder and handed him the pages. "Copies of invoices with the fake name we used to rent the villa."

He let out a long, low whistle. "I can't believe this," he said. "I would never have pegged Gina as the deceptive type."

"Me neither," she admitted as she pressed her fingertips against her temple. "David and Walter made me look like a complete fool. I was sitting there, insisting Gina was my friend, then David rams this down my throat. I was hoping Gina would meet me and have some plausible explanation for those."

Wesley pulled the bottom invoice from the stack. "It's pretty damning stuff. Especially this one."

She accepted the invoice dated the day before her father had found the flowers outside The Rose Tattoo. "They're all pretty damning."

"Look here," he said, tapping the logo in the corner. "This tulip matches the scrap Dylan and I found attached to the envelope."

"I guess that seals it," she said as she allowed the page to slip from her hand. "I can't believe I was such a fool. Gina and I have been friends for years."

"And you can't think of a single reason she might want to hurt you?"

"That's what's so puzzling about this," Destiny said as she folded her leg beneath her and shifted so that she faced him. "We've had a few disagreements, but nothing major. I can't think of a single reason she'd want to do something like this to me. I'm also having a hard time figuring out why she would go to the extreme of sticking a knife in her ribs."

"She couldn't have," Wesley said.

"We saw the blood, remember? I know it's crazy, but—"

"I'm telling you, it wasn't a self-inflicted wound." Conviction hung on every word.

"How do you know that?"

He flashed her that patient, sexy half smile that quickened her pulse and made the room feel suddenly warm.

"Your psychiatric training allows you to evaluate how a wound was inflicted?"

He blinked and sucked in a deep breath, holding it briefly before expelling it slowly. Destiny tried not to pay attention to the way his chest filled out, straining against the pale gray cotton shirt. Or the few dark hairs peeking out where he'd neglected to button the top few buttons.

"I worked in the ER for a few years."

"As a resident?"

"Yep," he said in a voice that was uncharacteristically tight. "And for a while afterward."

"After what? Don't you rotate from internship to internship while you're in school?"

"I graduated from medical school eight years ago."

"And you're just now getting around to taking your boards?"

"In a new area," he hedged. "I'm already board certified as a trauma surgeon."

"Are you telling me you were a surgeon and now you're changing gears?"

"Pretty much," he said with a shrug. "Which is why I can tell you with relative certainty that Gina's wound wasn't self-inflicted. The angle of entry was an upward thrust."

He got up, grabbing her hands and pulling her with him. "I'll demonstrate." Wesley took a sculpted marble banana from the arrangement on the coffee table and held it out for her. "This is a knife."

"It's a banana," she quipped. "Knives are long and sharp, not curved and yellow."

"Funny," he said through a mildly irritated smile. "*Pretend* this is a knife."

"Okay," she said, "but I think I'll have a hard time slicing through a tomato with this."

"Now, pretend you were going to stab your-self...right here."

Destiny flinched slightly when his fingers went to her rib cage, counting up from the bottom, leaving a heated path.

"Why am I doing this?"

"I'm conducting a demonstration."

That wasn't the only thing he was conducting, she thought as she closed her eyes and drank in the freshly washed scent of his hair as he poked and probed the indentation between her ribs.

"Okay, now. If you wanted to stab yourself where I'm holding my finger, show me how you'd do it."

"I wouldn't stab myself," she told him for some inane reason.

He glanced down at her, his mouth curved in an ex-asperated frown. "Stop being difficult."

Then stop touching me, she thought. Instead she simply said, "Okay. I'll play."

Destiny made an arching motion with her hand, thrusting the banana-knife to the place where his blunt-tipped finger rested at her side.

"See my point?" he asked.

"No pun intended?" Her brow lifted and she smiled up at him.

"Stay with the program," he said with a sigh. "If Gina stabbed herself for effect, the blade of the knife would have entered at a downward angle."

"But it didn't?"

He shook his head and took the marble banana out of her hand to place it against his own body. "Her wound was definitely at this angle." He positioned the mock weapon flat in his palm and indicated an impossibly awkward motion. "Unless she placed the knife in her hand like this, which doesn't make any sense, there's no way she stabbed herself."

"So, what does that mean?"

"I'm not sure yet," he admitted as he placed the banana back among the other faux fruit. "But it makes me wonder why your friends were in such a hurry to convince you that Gina is the culprit."

"They didn't make up the invoices," she said.

She watched as deep lines of concentration appeared around his mouth and eyes. "There's only one way to find out."

"Tell the police?"

"Not yet. I don't think you want them arresting Gina just yet."

"No," she agreed. "I don't want to do anything until I'm absolutely convinced."

ABSOLUTELY CONVINCED, he repeated in his brain as he turned into the alleyway next to The Rose Tattoo. Destiny had been very quiet during the ride, and a wariness dulled the unusual shade of her eyes. Wesley parked next to Susan's half-primer, half-green clunker.

"I hope my mother has saved us a few crumbs. You probably didn't eat much lunch."

Her only response was an absent shrug of her small shoulders. "It's quite fashionable to be thin these days."

"But you're about to do a couple of hours under the lights."

"Piece of cake," she assured him, pulling her smile into place like a protective shield. "The audience won't have a clue that I'm being jerked around by my closest friend."

She had been absolutely right, he decided as he sat at one of the small tables with his mother. Her timing was good, her jokes fresh, her smile breathtaking.

"Are you sleeping with her?"

Wesley gave his mother a shocked look.

Rose lifted her drink to her bloodred lips and took a small, dainty sip. It was an action at strict odds with her garish outfit. Her wardrobe never ceased to make him cringe. Tonight she'd poured herself into a second skin of black spandex and a low-cut leopard top. A collection of big bronze balls hung around her neck, matching the oversize earrings that reflected the flame of the candle. But, he thought as he recrossed his legs, it was Rose at her best.

"I know you haven't known her long, but it seems to me that you two are perfectly matched."

"She's a nice lady," he responded.

"Barbara Bush is a *nice* lady," Rose said. "Destiny Talbott has spirit."

And great legs, he thought as he watched her stroll across the stage. "Leave it alone," he warned without looking at his mother.

"I swear," Rose mumbled, "I can't believe my own sons are so afraid of commitment."

He regarded her out of the corner of his eye. "J.D. is disgustingly happily married. How do you figure he's afraid of commitment?"

Rose thrust out her bottom lip. "He'd still be single if it weren't for me."

"I think Tory would challenge you on that theory."

Wesley allowed his eyes to drift back to the woman on the stage. He wasn't really listening to her monologue—he'd heard it every night since her arrival. Instead, he studied each feature in turn. He remembered all too well how her hair looked, fanned out against his pillow. A groan rumbled and died in his throat as the memory of their shared passion filled his consciousness. He'd never experienced anything quite so intense as making love to Destiny Talbott. He frowned, unable to put a name on what he was feeling. There didn't seem to be a label that was appropriate for the magical, explosive, incredible way he felt when they were together. And it wasn't just the sex. He wasn't dumb enough to delude himself on that count. His feelings about her went beyond the physical. He couldn't be in the same room as her without seeking her out. He would gladly sit for hours just watching her, admiring.

"You're falling," Rose chirped in an annoying singsong voice.

"I don't know what you're talking about."

"Look at you," she said. "You stare at her like she's the first woman you ever laid eyes on. You definitely have the *look*."

"Wipe that grin off your face," Wesley warned. "There's nothing to grin about."

"Don't hand me that," Rose stated confidently. "I'm so excited."

He snarled, "You're hallucinating, Mother," as he watched her rub her hands together expectantly.

Rose shook her head vigorously but her heavily sprayed hair didn't budge. "It's in your eyes," Rose insisted. "I saw that same look in Shelby's eyes when she was around Dylan. J.D. had it whenever Tory was within a mile. Now you. This is wonderful. Finally, I'm going to get some grandchildren."

"You're going to get the cold shoulder if you don't stop spewing this nonsense. I like her, but that's as far as it's going to go."

He saw the flicker of compassion in his mother's green eyes. "You can't spend the rest of your life punishing yourself for what happened all those years ago. I'm sure your Linda wouldn't have wanted that."

"Drop it," he said as he raked his hand through his hair. He was annoyed with his mother for bringing up Linda's name. He was even more bothered that this was the first time he'd thought of Linda since meeting Destiny.

"DON'T BLAME ME," David implored.

"I'm not blaming you," she insisted as she twisted the telephone cord around her index finger. "I'm simply asking you to keep this to yourself for a few days."

"We should turn the information over to the cops immediately so they can start looking for her."

Destiny met Wesley's eyes and silently communicated her dilemma. He responded by taking the receiver from her hand.

"Hello, Crane," she heard him say in a tone that was anything but friendly. "I think you have to follow Destiny's lead on this one." There was a brief silence before he said, "That would be a big mistake. Give us twenty-four hours and then you can go tattle to your heart's content." Another pause and then, "Fine." Wesley passed the phone back to her.

"David, I—"

"Twenty-four hours, Destiny," he said. "One day, and then I'm going to do the right thing."

"Why are you in such a rush?" she pleaded. "You act like you're looking forward to throwing Gina to the wolves."

"I am," he told her flatly. "What she's been doing to you—to all of us—is inexcusable and she needs to be punished."

"Thank you, judge and jury," she retorted.

"C'mon, Destiny. I showed you the invoices. Gina's obviously gone off the deep end."

"Or she was pushed," she said in a near whisper before hanging up.

"Pushed into what?" Wesley asked as he refilled their coffee cups.

"I've been thinking. What if Gina was somehow manipulated into ordering those flowers?"

"Who would have the power to do that?"

"Power?"

He ran his fingertip around the rim of the mug. "In order to manipulate someone, you have to have some sort of power over them. A superior bargaining position."

"Me," Destiny answered. "I guess I had power over her, because I was her only source of income."

Tilting his head, he offered a kind smile. "I think we can rule you out as a possible suspect."

"You are a bright guy," she said with a smile and a playful wink.

"Attractive, too," he said.

"And humble."

He gave a theatrical sigh. "I can't be everything."

You're enough, she thought as her eyes dropped to view his broad chest. His shirt was open, allowing her to feast on the sight of well-developed muscle and richly tanned skin. The sight caused a lump to lodge in her throat. She took a sip of coffee, hoping to wash away the lump and the fantasies.

"Enough about me. What do you say we go and check in with the florist?"

"Us?"

His shoulders lifted. "Why not?"

"Right," she agreed, slapping her forehead. "What was I thinking? It makes perfect sense for a comedienne and a shrink to launch an investigation. What other credentials could we possibly need?"

"Have you always been such a defeatist?"

"I like to think of myself as practical."

"Boring."

She swatted at the hand he held out for her. "I am not boring," she told him with exaggerated hauteur.

"No," he said, his voice dropping to a husky invitation. "You're definitely not boring."

Taking her hands, Wesley gently pulled her up against him. His eyes went over her like hands, searching and intent. He drew in an uneven breath.

"Don't do this," she said in a shaky voice.

"Do what?" he asked as he captured a lock of her hair in his fingers and quietly studied it.

"This," she prompted. "I thought we agreed—"

"You agreed," he told her as his fingertip traced a path along her cheek. "I didn't argue at the time, because I didn't want you to leave."

His finger brushed her bottom lip.

"Why?"

His eyes fell to her mouth.

"Why what?"

"Why don't you want me to leave?"

Wesley's gentle exploration of her mouth stopped, and he lifted his gaze to hers. She saw a stormy mixture of conflicting emotions clouding his eyes. It was desire tempered by caution.

"Does it matter?" he asked. "Isn't it more important that I don't want you to leave?"

She was mesmerized by the deep hum of his voice. Lulled into complacency by the inviting promise of his mouth as it came down on hers.

She went warm and soft all over, relishing the feel of his strong body beneath her hands. His fingers framed her face as his lips touched hers, hesitantly at first, then more insistently when she leaned into him.

She felt the very instant his body stiffened, felt the sharp intake of breath when she invited him past the seam of her lips. He eased her back against the wall, pinning her there with a gentle, exquisite strength that only heightened the level of her response.

Destiny, once adamantly opposed to this, now found herself a willing participant. He said her name, causing a shuddering need to spill from the tight coil of her stomach. The feel of his body made her tingle from head to toe. His fingers stroked the curve of her throat as his tongue teased her sensitive mouth.

He moved away from her then, his hands resting on her upper arms. She felt drowsy and tense all at once.

"I can either ravish you here on the kitchen table," he suggested with a lecherous grin, "or we can stop now. Your call."

"Is there a column C?" she asked, pulling her bottom lip nervously between her teeth.

Wesley chuckled, a deep, wonderful sound that renewed the tiny shocks electrifying her nerve endings.

"Not this time," he said as he moved her to one side, his arm draped casually over her shoulder. "I think we should get organized and go check out the florist. Something tells me your buddy David won't wait a split second past the time limit."

"Give me a minute to paint my face."

"Your face doesn't need painting," he said against her ear.

"It's either paint or a bag," she said.

Destiny hurriedly applied a small amount of blusher to her cheekbones, followed by a dab of mascara and some clear gloss to her lips. Kissing Wesley had added a certain spark to her eyes, making her look alive and invigorated.

"Careful, girl," she told her reflection. "The guy only kissed you."

His words came back to her then, and she frowned when she realized it *did* matter. She *did* want to know why he'd asked her to stay. Unless, of course, it was for the obvious reason.

She groaned as she ran the brush through her hair. "Maybe he wants to keep you around because you seem to melt into his arms whenever he crooks his pinkie."

It wasn't a pleasant thought.

"Why the scowl?" he asked when she emerged from the bedroom a few minutes later.

"I don't like my dress," she lied.

"It's a nice dress. The color matches your eyes."

"It's an *okay* dress," she said. "And it's got a little too much pink to match my eyes."

"Did I miss something?" Wesley said as his fingers closed around her upper arm. His eyebrows drew together in a definite frown before he asked, "Why are you angry?"

"I'm not angry," she said as she gave her arm a futile tug. "We were discussing my dress."

He reached up and tucked her chin between his thumb and forefinger. A composed smile curved the corners of his mouth. "You're mad because we kissed."

"We shouldn't be kissing."

"I'm a man, you're a woman. We're genetically predisposed to kissing each other."

She peered up at him through her lashes. "You sound like a textbook again."

"Just stating one of the basics of human behavior."

"You're justifying *your* behavior."

"Our behavior," he corrected as his thumb grazed her skin. "I don't think I have to justify my behavior. We weren't doing anything wrong."

"Depends on your perspective," she answered, quoting him. "We shouldn't keep—"

His mouth came down on hers for just an instant. It was long enough to derail her train of thought. "You're complicating a very simple, straightforward act," he said.

Destiny didn't argue. She didn't think she could ever get Wesley to understand that kissing him was anything but simple.

They found the florist's shop in a strip mall on the road leading out to the beachfront resorts southeast of town. It was a small, narrow store, filled with both natural and artificial gift items. A sharp, shrill bell sounded when they closed the door.

The air was thick with the commingled fragrances of flowers, incense and potpourri. A tiny woman with delicate hands and a warm smile greeted them.

"May I help you?"

"I'm interested in this," Destiny said as she carefully unfolded the photocopy of the invoice and placed it on the counter next to the credit-card machine.

The woman picked up the pair of glasses dangling from a chain around her neck and placed them on the end of her nose. "The gardenias," she said with a smile. "Lovely blossom, but a bit heavy in this quantity."

"We'd like some information about the purchaser," Wesley said.

She looked up at them, her brown eyes just above the thick, half-moon lenses. "May I ask why?"

"I received the flowers," Destiny explained. "But I'm afraid I don't know who to thank."

The woman's features relaxed, and she reached under the counter and produced a tattered receipt book. "I remember taking this order over the phone," she said as she began to flip through the pages. "I only remember because it isn't every day we get an order for two dozen gardenias. Quite unusual."

"You don't know the half of it," Destiny said under her breath.

"Here it is," she announced as she turned the book toward them. "We filled the order the day it was placed."

"This matches the copy I brought in," Destiny told the woman.

She smiled with pride. "Of course it does. We faxed it to the customer for her records. I remember because it was the first time I used the fax machine all by myself."

"Where did you fax it to?" Wesley asked.

"Where?" The woman blinked.

"The number?" Destiny prodded. "A cover sheet? Something?"

"I never thought to save it," she admitted sheepishly. "Is it important?"

"Does your fax machine print a log?" Wesley asked.

The woman just stared at him, her eyes blank and uncomprehending. "Log?"

"May I see your machine?"

"It's in the office," she explained. "We don't allow customers behind the counter."

"Would you go and see if it has a button marked Log or Journal?" Wesley suggested.

"I can try," she said with a rather helpless little shrug. "But I'm not very good with machines."

"Wonderful," Destiny whispered as soon as the woman left the room. "Of all the small businesses in Charleston, we have to deal with the technologically challenged."

"Progress?" he suggested.

"This is supposed to be the age of the information highway. That woman," she said, tilting her head in the direction of the closed office door, "ought to get out of the fast lane."

"Patience," he warned. "I'm sure she'll come through."

After several long moments the woman came back, looking very frazzled and very apologetic. "Not only could I not find a log, I managed to erase our sender information from the console. Bernice will kill me."

"It's an easy thing to fix," Wesley assured her. "When do you expect Bernice?"

"She's in Florida. Her mother broke her hip in a fall."

"Is there any way we can find out where you sent that fax?" Destiny asked. "Do you remember any part of the telephone number?"

The woman shook her head. "I don't remember anything."

"What about the actual order?" Wesley asked.

She tapped her finger against her chin, apparently searching her memory. "It was a while ago," she hedged. "Most of our business is done over the phone."

"Do you remember the phone call?" Wesley asked.

"I remember she was very nice," she said. "Very exact about what she wanted."

Destiny felt her spirits fall to her feet. Gina had a lovely telephone presence. She felt Wesley's hand at the small of her back, and she leaned into him, drawing on his strength.

"What arrangements did she make for the flowers?" he asked.

"She wired the payment immediately after the call."

"Wired the payment?" Destiny repeated. "No credit card?"

Destiny took the invoice and pointed to the name and address written at the top. "My manager found this among the accounts receivable. Are you telling me it's already been paid?"

She nodded, "Absolutely. I must have just forgotten to mark the bill paid. Sorry."

"What arrangements did she make for the flowers?"

"That was a little strange," she admitted. "It's the only time I've ever delivered flowers to a gas station."

"Excuse me?"

"As soon as we received the wire, we sent Fred out with the delivery. He took them to the service station on Bay Street, north of the Battery."

"Can we talk to Fred?" Wesley asked.

"He only works mornings this week. He's a house painter. He's got another job going right now."

"What time might we be able to catch him in the morning?" Wesley asked.

"Around nine," she answered, her eyes growing narrow and suspicious. "The purchaser's name is right here on the invoice. Why are you asking me all these questions? I thought you said you didn't know who sent you the flowers."

"I don't," Destiny said. "The name on the invoice isn't correct."

"Well," she insisted, her posture defensive, "it's the name she gave me. I remember that clear as a bell."

"Didn't Tiffany Glass sound a bit...phony to you?" Wesley asked gently.

She shrugged. "All I know is that I wrote it just like she spelled it. She had to spell it on account of her speech impediment."

"What kind of speech impediment?"

"She had a lisp. And a pretty heavy accent."

"Spanish? German? What?"

The woman shook her head. "New York, New Jersey. One of those Yankee accents."

Chapter Fourteen

"Why is it that every time I get off a major highway someone is waiting to sell me flowers?" Destiny allowed for the chuckle of recognition. "I don't know about you guys, but I don't usually have major romantic longings when I'm exiting a major thoroughfare."

During the brief pause, she recognized Wesley's outline beyond the lights. Just knowing he was there made her feel safe and confident as she continued her performance.

"I have a friend who's a surgeon. Do any of you know the difference between God and a surgeon?"

Several patrons yelled, "No!"

"God doesn't practice medicine," she said with a sly grin. "Thanks very much, you've been great!"

SHE WAS FLAUNTING IT in front of everyone, he thought as his fingers tightened around the half-empty glass. A doctor, he fumed. It had to be him. He glared at the back of the tall man's head.

They couldn't fool him. He'd seen them together, followed them to that ritzy building overlooking the *harbor. But he wasn't the one for Destiny. The doctor didn't understand her the way he did.*

Slipping his hand inside his jacket, he felt the cool handle of the knife protruding from the thin leather strap. Maybe he would kill them both, just to teach them a lesson.

The doctor moved then, turning his face in profile. The sight of his jovial expression tightened the knot in his churning stomach. He had no reason to be so happy. Didn't he understand that Destiny was using him, just as she used everyone? If the doctor was dumb enough to be taken in by her lying ways, he deserved to die.

Destiny made her exit then, the applause that followed her from the stage fuel for his burning anger. He gripped the knife more tightly, his mind fragmented by the deafening noise. The audience was disturbing his thoughts, and it was all her fault.

Lifting the glass to his lips, he drained the contents and savored the burning path left by the Scotch. His eyes scanned the room, searching for the woman they called Gina. That one had thwarted him on more than one occasion. He mentally added her to his list of potential victims. She deserved to die for interrupting his efforts. Yes, he thought as a cruel smile tugged at his lips. The doctor and Gina should die, and Destiny would watch while he did it.

"DOCTOR JOKES?" Wesley asked, one dark brow raised disapprovingly.

"What can I say?" She sighed as she sank farther into the rich leather of the bucket seat. "I've never been able to turn down a good straight line." *I've also never been able to turn you down,* she added as she chanced a peek at him.

They'd fallen into a rather comfortable pattern. So comfortable that Destiny actually expected to be escorted to and from the club by the handsome man driving the car. They shared meals, thoughts, conversation and sex.

"Why the frown?"

"Just replaying my act. Working out the bugs."

"I didn't hear any bugs," he said as his hand slipped across the console and covered hers. "I'm amazed by the way you change the routine every night."

"It encourages repeat business," she explained, trying not to think about the way his thumb was gently brushing her knuckles.

Wesley turned into the parking lot of his building, but the guard didn't immediately open the gate. Tilting her head, Destiny peered out at the uniformed man in the booth. "Are you behind on your condo fees?" she quipped.

He gave her a sidelong glance before cracking the window. Wesley said, "Hi, Fred. Is the gate stuck?"

"Evening, Dr. Porter. Miss Talbott," he answered with a broad grin. "Got something for you," he stated before he dipped low in the booth, reminding her of the opening credits of "Get Smart." He reappeared and hoisted a loosely wrapped item toward them.

Wesley cursed under his breath. Destiny simply stared, paralyzed by the unexpected shock.

Moving quickly, he got out and grabbed the package from the guard. The action was enough to ruffle the wrapping, allowing a small plastic hand to slip free. She watched as he opened the trunk, then after a second slammed it with a reverberating thud.

Wesley exchanged a few hushed words with the guard before he returned to the car. "I'll call Greavy and Dylan as soon as I get you upstairs," he said, his eyes filled with apology, kindness and shimmering anger.

"How would he know to send a doll here?"

"Gina knows where you are," he said gently. "It was delivered by messenger, addressed to you."

Sighing, she closed her eyes and shook her head sadly. "I guess this puts Gina at the top of our suspect list. I only wish I knew why."

Wesley was quiet as they ascended in the elevator. There was a preoccupied look in his eyes and an unyielding hardness to his tight expression.

"You're acting as if this is happening to you," she said as soon as they were safely inside.

"It is," he said simply.

She followed him into the living room and remained quiet as he made the calls. Her eyes were fixed on the unwrapped doll. Even morbid curiosity wasn't enough to make her touch the thing.

"Dylan and Greavy will be here soon," he told her as he draped his arm over her shoulder. "Do you want some tea? Or something stronger?"

"I don't do stronger," she said, forcing lightness into her voice.

"Probably a good idea. Tea, then?"

"Soda. Diet, if you have it."

He stopped in midstride, turning her with his hands braced on her shoulders. "Are you okay? I remember what happened the last time you got a delivery."

She shrugged and studied the small white button on his shirt. "I'm afraid. First he manages to get within a few feet of me at The Rose Tattoo. Now he leaves a little something for me here. I'd be lying if I said I wasn't scared."

He folded her against him, gently stroking her hair. "I'll make sure nothing happens to you."

"You keep forgetting you may not have any say in the matter."

"I still don't see Gina as a real threat to your safety. It just doesn't feel right."

"I know. I can't even imagine Gina hurting me in a physical way. But I—"

"Hush," he commanded softly. "I may not know Gina as well as you do, but I'd stake my life on my belief that she's being set up."

She stepped back and met his eyes, clutching his shirt. "Do you really believe that?"

"Absolutely." His finger fell below her chin, delicately raising her face to his. "There's something else going on here."

He emphasized one of them as he lowered his mouth to cover hers. It was very different from the other kisses they had shared. This was tractable, docile and tender. It was nothing like the passionate, needful, heated kisses from the past. He was infinitely gentle as his tongue teased her lips. His arms wrapped around her, cradling her in his arms.

The contrast was stunning and confusing. She'd come to expect thought-shattering passion. She wasn't the least bit prepared for this unexpected display of patient sensitivity. His actions tugged at her heart and planted a dangerous seed in her mind.

Wesley's fingers circled her waist, but he made no move to pull her against him. His mouth continued to do delectable things to hers. The considerate way he was kissing her made her feel as if she was being cherished by a man who knew what he was doing.

And then it was over. He held her eyes with his. What she saw in those clear blue depths was even more confounding than the tone of his kiss. He searched her face quietly, looking very much as if he wanted to say something. He didn't.

"Thanks," she said nervously. "I needed that."

"Me, too," he said on a breath. Then he smiled and winked, erasing the turbulence in his eyes.

She watched him as he set about the task of pouring her drink. A small warning penetrated her thoughts. What was happening between them? Why had Wesley made her his responsibility? Why did he kiss her until her toes curled? More importantly, why had he just kissed her like *that*? As if he was acting on more than just a generous amount of testosterone?

An urgent knock at the door forced her to abandon her contemplation. Plastering a smile on her face, she remained perched on the bar stool while Wesley ushered a rather haggard-looking Dylan into the room.

They filled him in on what she had learned from Walter, David and the ditsy woman at the florist shop.

Dylan raked long fingers through his black hair. His eyes shone through narrow, troubled slits. "Was there a note with the doll you got tonight?"

Wesley shook his head. "I only tore the paper. I didn't go hunting around underneath."

Dylan nodded as soon as he read the neatly typed block letters on the note he held in his hand. "Nothing new, then," he stated. "What about the guard? Does he remember anything about the delivery? Maybe he can ID the person who dropped it off?"

"No truck," Wesley explained. "It arrived by limo."

"What?" Destiny asked, incredulous.

Wesley moved next to her, placing a comforting hand on her shoulder. It was so natural, so right that she crooked her neck and rested her cheek against his hand. Drinking in the scent of soap, she breathed deeply, contented.

"A limo pulled up and the driver just dumped it with the guard."

Dylan hooked his thumbs through the belt loops of his jeans. "Dead end."

"Why is that?" she asked.

"Anyone with cash can rent a limo. It's an expensive but safe way to get the job done."

"Then it can't be Gina," Destiny said firmly. "She doesn't have the money to go around hiring limos."

"Maybe she charged it to you," Dylan suggested. "Have you thought of canceling your charge cards? Cutting off the access?"

"I'll take care of it in the morning. It's pretty depressing to think I might be paying for all this torment."

"You should be more than depressed," Dylan told her, his expression serious. "Whoever is behind this is too close. I think it's time for you to go into hiding."

Lifting her head, Destiny pleaded with her eyes. "There has to be another way."

"Unfortunately," Wesley said as he gave her a small, reassuring squeeze, "this is one of the few instances when the victim is responsible for her own safety."

"But I've called the police."

"I know," Wesley replied as he moved to stand in front of her. "But Dylan's right. The police can't protect you, and..." He paused, taking in a long, frustrated breath. "I don't think I can, either. Whoever is behind this isn't going to be deterred by me."

"He's right," Dylan interjected. "Your stalker won't mind going through Wesley to get to you."

"But I haven't done anything wrong," she cried, struggling against a sudden flash of angry tears. "If I run and hide, he wins."

"If you don't, you could die." Wesley's soft warning came out with a small warble of emotion. "And it's about time you faced the reality of all this."

"Which is?"

Wesley took her hands in his and held them against his chest. She could feel the rapid beat of his heart and see the defeat in his eyes.

"Even if they catch this guy, he won't be imprisoned forever."

"What are you saying?"

"He'll serve a year, maybe two. Statistically speaking, he'll do his time and then pick up where he left off."

"You're joking," she said, her eyes wide, disbelieving.

Wesley lowered his eyes, then said, "It's a very high probability. It's time to face facts, Destiny."

"Which facts?"

"Life as you know it is over."

Chapter Fifteen

Destiny stood in the shadows at the back of the club, her eyes fixed on the empty stage. Her whole body felt heavy as the reality of her predicament began to sink in. Dylan and Wesley had argued with her until the wee hours of the morning. Frustration surged through her and she kicked the leg of one of the tables in a childish attempt to release some of her rage.

"Rose said you were in here."

Destiny jumped at the sound of the voice.

"I didn't mean to scare you," Shelby said with an apologetic smile. "But I have a feeling you're probably afraid of your own shadow at this point."

Destiny nodded. "I'm a heartbeat away from losing my grip."

Shelby took two chairs off one of the tables and pushed one toward her. "I know *exactly* how you feel."

"Dylan's obsessed with you, but I don't think he's dangerous."

"Dylan's great," she said, genuine affection in her voice. "But he wasn't the one who tormented me."

"You, too?" Destiny gasped, leaning forward. "I

thought I was the only one with a deadly secret admirer.''

"My experience wasn't exactly like what you're going through," Shelby clarified. "When my son was kidnapped, I received . . . calls.''

Destiny saw plainly the pain and residual fear in Shelby's eyes. "But everything worked out for you.''

Shelby nodded. "Thank God. I was lucky. The men tormenting me weren't doing it for personal reasons.''

"It's wonderful to be loved," Destiny said. "I just wish I knew *why* this guy is so obsessed with me.''

"That's the hardest part," Shelby agreed. "That, and knowing you have absolutely no control over your own life.''

"That's an understatement." Destiny sighed. "I don't know what I'm going to do.''

"You have to put your safety first.''

"I know that," Destiny said in a strangled voice. "I'm just not sure I can give all this up. I've worked my tail off for almost fifteen years to get this close.''

Shelby patted her hand. "And maybe you'll still get there, but you can't jeopardize yourself, or Wesley. . . .''

"Hanging around was his idea," Destiny told her. "For some reason he's determined to play knight in shining armor. I think it has something to do with atoning for a past sin.''

"It does.''

Destiny met the other woman's eyes, issuing a silent request.

"It isn't my place to tell you what drives Wesley. I can only promise you that there's more to it than simple atonement.''

"What's that supposed to mean?"

Shelby shifted uncomfortably. "I really think Wesley should be the one to tell you—"

"The only thing Wesley tells me is the way to the bedroom," she interrupted. "He's kind, decent, fun, intelligent and completely secretive about himself."

Shelby smiled. "He is that."

"He's a lot of things," she responded, mostly to herself.

"This is more complicated than I thought," Shelby observed. "You're falling for him, aren't you?"

Destiny slumped back in her seat and folded her hands in her lap. "I don't know what I'm doing. Maybe what I'm feeling for him is just a knee-jerk reaction to my current situation. I'm scared, he's strong. You know the drill."

"I know what it's like to turn to someone for comfort," Shelby said earnestly. "I also know that there are many elements to comfort. You might need Wesley's strength right now, or you might just need him."

"Except that he doesn't impress me as the sort of man who needs any woman. He's all but said as much."

"Saying and doing are two entirely different things. Especially when we're talking about the male of the species."

Destiny laughed. "Amazing creatures, men. So much potential and so little follow-through."

"The good ones follow through," Shelby said as she got up. "I've got to get back. I left Chad with Susan. She's probably reading his palm and adjusting his aura."

Destiny shook her head. "Not today. Today your resident mystic is into numerology. I'm a seven."

"Great." Shelby sighed. "She has her work cut out for her with my son. He can't even grasp the concept of counting."

"He's only two. His DNA will kick in soon, and he'll probably graduate from college before his twelfth birthday."

"Only if he's potty trained."

Shelby started to leave when Destiny called her name. "Thanks," she said softly. "I appreciate the pep talk."

"Anytime."

Shelby was harassed and lived through it, she told herself as she wandered closer to the stage. Her footsteps echoed in the still of the room. She was concentrating on the sound when she heard another. The sound of the door opening.

"Forget someth . . ."

The words died in her throat when she turned and saw the hooded figure slither into the building. Panic welled up inside her and she fought to contain it.

"We're not open yet," she called, holding her voice steady.

"It's time, my Destiny."

That ice-cold, emotionless voice chilled her blood. Automatically she took a half step back, her mind whirling with possible options. *Stay calm.*

"I know you've been expecting me," he said, his words amplified in the deserted building. "You shouldn't have taken up with that doctor."

"Look," she began, trying to keep the panic out of her voice. "I'm sure you're right, and we definitely need to talk about this—"

"I tried that!" he shouted. "You wouldn't take my calls. You didn't answer my letters, either."

She continued her slow, cautious movement toward the stage. "I'm really bad at writing letters," she apologized. Her heart began to beat erratically and she found it increasingly difficult to catch her breath. *Not again,* she prayed silently.

"You're just bad, Destiny," he growled, taking that first threatening step.

Thanks to the hood of his sweatshirt she couldn't make out his face. She could, however, see the shining reflection of the knife in his left hand. Her breathing became short and erratic. Her eyes darted around the room, seeking an escape. He stood in front of the only door.

"I'm sorry for whatever I did—"

"It's too late for apologies. I gave you your chance. Now you have to pay for your sins."

"Which sins were those?" she asked. He didn't move when he talked and she hoped to buy time.

"You've made me a laughingstock. You cost me my job."

Destiny listened to the voice. She didn't recognize it. "I'm sorry about your job, Mr.—"

"You should be. They teased me. Made it impossible for me to keep working."

"What kind of work do you do?" She felt the edge of the stage bite into her back. It was only a matter of precious seconds before she'd have to make her move.

"I told you in my letters."

"Tell me again. I really want to know."

"You've run out of room, my Destiny," he said, sneering and moving closer.

Destiny let out a bloodcurdling scream and bolted to the left. Slamming through the stage entrance, she shoved aside the curtains leading backstage.

It was pitch-black and she hoped that would give her an advantage. Keeping herself flat against the wall, she hurried toward her dressing room, all the while taunted by the sound of pursuing footsteps.

She found the entrance and threw herself into the room, then slammed and bolted the lock. The pain in her chest was excruciating. The pressure had taken her breath, and she was already seeing flashes of starlike light before her eyes.

He reached the door just a few seconds later, and there was a resounding thud. Apparently he was battering the door with his stocky body.

The hinges rattled and she watched in silent horror as the metal plate of the lock began to give way.

The phone! she remembered as she ran and crashed against the makeup table. Several things broke, and glass shattered to accompany her tormentor's second attempt to tear down the door.

Destiny was gasping for breath as she struggled to dial the number.

Josh, the bartender, got it on the second ring.

"Help me," she cried. "Destiny. In the dependency. Call cops."

"Destiny?"

"Help me," she managed to choke out just as the walls and door rattled from another onslaught. "Help me!"

"Destiny?" The familiar voice came on the line.

"Wes . . . ley. Here . . . almost . . . here."

"In the club?"

"Yes."

She heard the sound of the receiver being dropped, and closed her eyes. Like a scared animal she backed behind the screen, fell to the ground and sat in a ball, her hands covering her ears. Then she heard it. The unmistakable sound of the doorframe shattering. But he wouldn't have to kill her—she was already dying. Her head began to swim as the lack of oxygen finally sent her over the precipice into oblivion.

As SHE OPENED HER EYES, the fear came back in a rush. Reflexively she struggled against the strong arms holding her. "Please let me go," she pleaded.

"It's okay, sweetheart. You're safe."

"Wesley?" She scrambled to a sitting position. "He was here. He was—"

"We got him."

She blinked and her mouth dropped open. "It's over?" she asked.

The smile he offered was answer enough. He helped her to her feet, holding her against him in the process. It was only then that she saw the prone form on the floor just outside the shattered doorframe.

"What happened to him?" she asked. "No, wait, who is he first?"

"No ID," Wesley answered.

"Wait," she said, hesitantly going over for a closer look at the man's now exposed face. "I don't believe it."

"You know him?"

"He's the man Gina and I told you about. The guy I said was harmless. Even Gregory talked to him and decided he was okay."

Rose appeared then, looking very harried as she gingerly stepped over the unconscious man. "Are you all right? The cops are on their way."

Destiny looked up into his eyes and said, "You did that?"

"Don't worry." He shrugged almost shyly. "He'll live." Wesley took her by the hand and passed her over to his mother. "Take her over to the restaurant. I'll keep an eye on him until the cops arrive."

Rose ushered her through the bustle of the kitchen. They went up to her office just as the wail of sirens penetrated the quiet of the back staircase.

Rose deposited her in a chair and went over to the small refrigerator tucked in the corner. "I have some decent brandy."

"I don't drink," she mumbled as she brushed some strands of hair away from her face.

"Wine, then?" Rose suggested. "You look as if you could use some fortification, girl."

"I don't think anything short of a steel rod in my spine could fortify me at this point."

"What *exactly* happened?"

"He just appeared."

"I thought Wesley told you to stay put."

"I misbehaved," she admitted. "I've been known to ignore directives in the past."

Rose deposited a glass of wine in front of her, then took the seat behind her desk. The older woman studied her with knowing green eyes.

"He didn't hurt you?"

She shook her head. "I had what your son refers to as a panic attack. Second one this week. I think it's becoming a habit."

"It's no wonder," Rose said as she took a sip of her wine. "You must be near your wit's end."

"I was," she acknowledged. "But thanks to your son, my life can now get back to normal."

"What does he get out of it?"

"Excuse me?"

One of her perfectly shaped eyebrows arched upward. "It seems to me you owe my son a debt of honor."

"I'm aware of that."

"How do you expect to repay him?"

"I haven't given it much thought."

"Then I'd like to offer a suggestion."

She regarded the woman, wary after Wesley's stories about the manipulative side of her flamboyant personality.

"Such as?"

"Stay with him until you finish your engagement here."

Destiny laughed aloud. "Under what pretext? I can't very well impose on the man."

"You wouldn't be imposing," Rose insisted.

"How do you know that?"

"Because I know my son. And I know he's in love with you."

Chapter Sixteen

Rose believed he loved her. Of course, she also believed there was an outside chance that Elvis was alive and hiding in Hoboken, Destiny reminded herself as she sat in the deserted office.

"You don't fall in love in less than a week," she said in a soft voice as she moved to the window overlooking the street. Tourists moved along the street, many clutching guide maps or cameras. Dusk was settling over Charleston, just as something undeniable was settling over her.

She was thrilled to know the police had carted off that awful man, but still she felt weighted by an unexplainable sadness. "I should be jumping for joy," she told herself as she fingered the edge of the curtain. "Maybe those panic attacks were just the first symptom of a complete and total nervous breakdown."

"I doubt that."

She turned slowly to find him filling the entrance to the office. At first glance she thought his guarded posture might be the result of recent events. Then she saw the caution in his eyes. His normally relaxed body seemed tense, almost coiled, like a snake caught in the indecision of the strike.

Destiny forced a smile to her lips. "If the panic attacks aren't enough, I've also taken to having long, meaningful talks with myself."

He shrugged. "You're a decent conversationalist."

"That sounds like classic rationalization."

"Now which one of us sounds like a textbook?"

"Point," she conceded. Relief washed over her when he smiled. "Do the police know who he is and why he was after me?"

Wesley shook his head. The action caused a lock of his hair to fall forward and she fought the urge to reach out and brush it back into place.

"He isn't talking."

"I guess it doesn't matter." She sighed, moving out from behind the desk. "As long as he's in jail, I don't care if he remains mute forever."

"Destiny." He said her name on an ominous whisper. It took him two strides to reach her. With one hand on her shoulder, he placed the other at the side of her throat.

She loved the feel of his hands, but she hated that look in his eyes. It held the promise of something bad.

"They're going to arrest him for trespassing."

"Very funny," she countered. But he wasn't laughing. He wasn't smiling, either. "You're serious, aren't you?"

"Unfortunately, he didn't actually *do* anything to you."

"But . . . the dolls . . . the notes. Surely—"

He placed his finger to her lips. "I know it doesn't seem right, but they can only charge him for acts committed."

"But he threatened me."

"I know that, baby," he soothed. "But knowing it and proving it in front of a judge are two entirely different things."

She closed her eyes and allowed her head to fall forward. Her forehead rested against his solid chest. "So now what am I supposed to do?"

"They can hold him for twenty-four hours. If he can make bail, he'll be out by morning."

"I don't believe this," she murmured against his shirt. "We finally catch him and he's going to get nothing but a little slap on the wrist."

"Look on the bright side," he suggested as he cupped her face in his hands. "At least you know for certain that Gina had nothing to do with this."

"You're right, but it's still kind of like saying 'Aside from that, Mrs. Lincoln, what did you think of the play?'" Destiny looked up at him through her lashes. "That guy was definitely the stalker," she told him. "He blamed me for everything but the Kennedy assassination." She shivered. "I've never had anyone speak to me with such venom before. His voice was—"

Wesley silenced her with his mouth. It was the kind of kiss she expected from him. It was forceful and demanding, highly charged and positively erotic. He did incredible things to the soft recesses of her mouth. Teased her with nothing more than the hint of what could be.

She clung to him, immersing herself in the feel of his body, the scent of his skin, the slightly abrasive stubble on his chin. Her body reacted powerfully, filling with desire too intense to be denied.

He groaned when she slipped her arms around his waist, resting her fingers against the slope of his lower back. Boldly she molded him against her, wanting to feel evidence that his need was as consuming as her own.

"What do you think my mother would say if I threw you down on top of her desk?"

"I'd tell you to lock the door first."

They flew apart, looking very much like teenagers caught necking on the porch.

"Sorry," Wesley said to his mother.

Rose shook her head. "Don't apologize to me. Apologize to her for not finishing what you started."

Destiny was so embarrassed that she dropped her eyes and focused on the wooden plank floor, while her cheeks continued to burn with shame.

"Don't you worry about my ability to finish what I start," Wesley told his mother easily. "You should be more concerned about promoting such behavior in your offspring."

"The fruit of my womb is a grown man," Rose stated. "I expect him to act like one. Which I believe includes all the usual needs and desires."

"I can't do this," Destiny said under her breath. "I'm mortified enough without listening to you two discuss..."

"Sex?" they said in unison.

"I'm going downstairs," Destiny announced as she fled the scene.

The restaurant was virtually empty, caught in the twilight between lunch and dinner. Dragging herself up on a stool, she glanced at her reflection in the mirror behind the bar. "Ugh," she groaned as she attempted to straighten her hair with her fingernails.

"You look fine to me," Josh said as he slipped a napkin across the bar. "I imagine you'd like something strong after all the fun at the club."

"Just a soda," she told him. "Diet."

"Anything the lady wants," Josh said easily.

She smiled at his outrageous flirting. Unfortunately for the libidinous bartender, she'd been forewarned. Josh returned with her drink and made another valiant attempt to draw her into conversation. Destiny was polite but firm. Josh was persistent. So persistent that she took her drink and went out to the side porch.

The air was heavy with humidity, thick with the threat of impending rain. She sat in one of the high-back rattan chairs and casually propped her feet on another. Leisurely, she sipped the soda and listened to snippets of passing conversation from the street below.

"Destiny?"

"Gina?" she responded, mimicking the urgent whisper of her friend.

"Down here."

Destiny went over to the railing and looked down into the alleyway. She saw nothing.

"Over here," Gina called out as she edged around the protective cover of the vegetable crates lining the alley.

"Come on up—"

"Be quiet," Gina implored. Her head turned from side to side, scanning the nearly dark alley. "Come down here. We have to talk."

Destiny walked around the front of the building, then backtracked. It was amazing how easy it was to walk among the tourists now that she no longer had to fear the stalker.

The alley was creepy, shadowed on one side by a large overgrowth of some sort of flowering vine.

She felt Gina's hand grip her arm, and she was unceremoniously tugged behind a stack of boxes. "Will you stop it?" Destiny hissed. "There's no need for all this secrecy. They caught the guy about an hour ago."

Gina's features were obscured by the poor light. "You have to listen to me," Gina urged, her voice filled with anxiety. "It isn't over."

"Trust me. I was in the dependency feeling incredibly sorry for myself when—"

"I was sending the flowers."

"Very funny," Destiny said with a grunt. "I know it wasn't you. Aren't you listening? They caught the guy. He was the one you kept telling me was suspicious. I'm sorry I didn't take your—"

"Destiny," Gina interjected, "I'm telling you that I *was* the one sending the flowers."

"Why are you doing this?" she asked.

"I'm trying to come clean. It wasn't until after the attack that I figured out this wasn't just a game."

"Let's go inside," Destiny suggested.

"No. I'm not staying. I just wanted you to know that I had no idea what he was doing. I don't know what he's told you, but I would never agree to do anything to hurt you. You have to believe me."

Destiny's mind was spinning. "Slow down, Gina. This isn't making any sense. Start from the beginning."

Gina leaned against the wall, and Destiny heard her suck in a fortifying breath before she said, "I didn't actually send the flowers, but I let them know where you were staying."

"Who?"

"That's just it," Gina cried. "I'm not certain."

"You did this to me at the request of a total stranger?" Destiny demanded. "You helped that crazy man. You should have heard him when he had me alone in the club."

"I never dealt with a man," Gina said quietly.

"Well, the guy who just got his clock cleaned by Wesley was definitely a man."

"I only spoke with a woman."

"Who was she?"

"I don't know."

"Which brings me back to my original question. Why were you helping someone you didn't know?"

"Stupidity, self-preservation," Gina answered. "I was afraid of what might happen to me. And she assured me she just wanted to get your attention. Nothing too traumatic. I thought I could keep them a secret. I thought I could intercept them, and you'd never be the wiser."

"So that was why you didn't tell me when the first flowers arrived."

"You never would have known about the flowers if David had watched for deliveries like I told him to. Believe me, Destiny. I never meant for you to even see those silly things."

Shrugging out of her friend's grasp, Destiny took in several calming breaths. "The flowers, the notes, the dolls. I can't—"

"That's what I've been trying to tell you," Gina interrupted. "I didn't have anything to do with the dolls. I don't know where they're coming from."

"Maybe your mystery woman found another courier."

"David, probably," Gina suggested.

"Just because you were willing to stab me in the back doesn't mean David would do the same."

"You have every right to be mad, Destiny. But think about it. I was the one who got stabbed. Whoever is after you wanted to make darn sure I wasn't around to tell what I know."

Destiny let out an exasperated sigh. "You haven't *told* me anything. Like why."

"She had pictures."

"Pictures of what?"

"Pictures I had taken when I was desperate. Pictures I was told had been destroyed three years ago."

"Pictures of the accident?"

"No. They were taken when I was very young and very, very stupid. I needed the money for a portfolio, so I did them."

The light began to dawn. "Dirty pictures?" Destiny asked.

"Filthy," Gina admitted. "I wasn't all there when I had them taken, either. That's how they rope you in. They give you a few pills to relax, then the day becomes a blur, and the next thing you know, you're the star of some pretty disgusting, pretty graphic stuff."

"And this woman had copies?"

"When she first approached me over the phone, I told her to go to hell."

"Then she sent you a little incentive?"

"I can't tell you what a shock it was to see those things resurface now. Look, Destiny," Gina began hesitantly. "The pictures would have hurt you, too."

"Hurt me more than finding out my friend has been torturing me?"

"They could have ruined you."

"I'm not in them," Destiny reasoned.

"But the implication might have destroyed you with the networks. I wasn't alone in the photographs," Gina said, her voice quivering. "There was another woman in the shots."

"I don't need to know any more."

"You and I are often photographed together. I was afraid that if the pictures were published, the obvious rumor might wreck your shot at the sitcom."

Destiny hung her head and tried to sort through this complicated mess. "I wish you had come to me."

"I wanted to, but by the time I got up my nerve, you'd seen one of the cards."

"So I guess this means that hideous little man in custody has a female partner."

"I don't think so," Gina said. "The night I was stabbed? It was dark in the room, so I guess he thought I was you and he asked me how I liked the doll."

"Those were *really* cruel," Destiny insisted, feeling her emotions come back to the surface. "Flowers are one thing, but those gruesome dolls were horrible. How could you do that to me?"

"That's what I've been trying to explain," Gina cried. "I don't know anything about the dolls!"

Chapter Seventeen

"She said what?"

"She wasn't behind the dolls," she told him as they sat in his darkened living room. He could gladly have wrung her neck for saving this bombshell until after the show.

"She said she didn't know anything about the dolls until the man who attacked her at the villa said something."

"But she was definitely the one behind the flowers."

Destiny nodded as she twisted her hair into a knot and tucked it up on her head. "And she only did that to protect me."

"Sending threatening notes is some way of protecting a friend."

"It's complicated," Destiny admitted as she tucked one leg under the other. "And I was mad at first, but then I started thinking about what she was saying. We need to talk to Mackie, the guy the police have in custody. Obviously, he's been working with someone."

Wesley felt his lips draw together in a pensive line. "That would be highly unlikely. Mackie isn't talking."

"But Gina said her only contact was a woman. And..." She leaned closer to him. Close enough so that he caught the subtle scent of her perfume. "Gina said the woman had a speech impediment and a thick Jersey accent."

He rolled his head around on his tense shoulders. "You're adding two and two and getting five."

He watched as some of the enthusiasm drained from her vibrant violet eyes. "Excuse me, Joe College. No doubt you're willing to leap into the breach and show me the error of my ways."

"David has the cops out looking for Gina. Remember his twenty-four-hour ultimatum?"

Destiny cursed and reached for the phone. David answered on the third ring. "I can't believe you sicced the police on Gina," she told him without preamble.

"I warned you."

"You made a mistake, David. I've spoken to Gina and she told me everything."

"I'll bet."

She ignored his sarcasm. "The man they arrested last night has a partner. A woman."

"Yeah," David agreed with a mirthless laugh. "Gina."

"Gina didn't have anything to do with the dolls. There has to be someone else involved."

"Do you have any proof?"

Destiny thought for a minute, then said, "The invoices you found. They were all receipts for flowers, nothing for dolls."

"I didn't find them."

"What?" she cried. "But you had them at lunch and I—"

"Walter gave them to me."

"Walter?" she repeated, feeling an uneasiness seep into her consciousness. "How did Walter get copies of my accounts?"

"He didn't say and I didn't ask."

"Well, I will," Destiny promised him.

"He's gone. He went back to D.C. right after our luncheon."

"That's why God invented the telephone."

After slamming down the receiver, she filled Wesley in on the developments. "I'll call him first thing in the morning."

He studied her quietly, then asked, "Just what is it you hope to learn from your patron saint?"

"An explanation. Something that will lead me to the woman with the speech impediment and the Jersey accent."

"Then what?" he asked as he moved closer to her.

"Are you asking me about my future plans?"

"I guess."

Tilting her head, she studied his serious expression. "You want me to tell you about my future when you haven't breathed a word about your past."

His head inclined slightly. "It isn't something that's easy for me to talk about. I'm not sure you'll want to hear it. I don't think you'll like me too much."

"Try me," she suggested as she placed her hand over his.

"I was engaged to an incredible woman when I was chief resident at Med Star in D.C."

"Great hospital," Destiny ventured.

His sad smile failed to reach his eyes. "ER doctors work some pretty hellacious shifts."

"So I've heard."

Raking his hands through his hair, Wesley averted his eyes before he continued with his story. "Linda was a teacher, totally devoted to her third-grade class."

"She sounds like a very nice person."

"She was more than nice—she had the ability to put me above the needs of her job. Even her own personal wants and desires."

"She sounds like a saint."

Closing his eyes, he sighed. "She was so understanding that I neglected her. Eventually I killed her."

"Come again?" she requested gently.

"I was so focused on being the greatest surgeon in the history of the world that I let every other aspect of my life take a back seat to my career."

His words struck a chord with Destiny. "Sometimes the only way to see success is to wear blinders."

His mouth curved into a half smile. "Confucius?"

"Mona Talbott," she admitted. "My mother is never caught without a pearl of wisdom. She's brilliant from the bench."

"Linda never complained. Not when I missed birthdays or holidays. Not even when I was away from home for days at a time."

"Your work required it."

He shook his head. "I went above and beyond the call of duty. I'd work my shift and stick around afterward just in case something interesting came through the ER."

"That tells me you were dedicated."

"I was self-absorbed, and Linda paid the ultimate price for my actions."

"How?"

"I was trying to make some points with the head of emergency services, so I spent a month working double shifts, sleeping at the hospital. Your basic brown-nosing." He slumped forward and pressed the pads of his fingertips together.

She could see the tension in his broad shoulders and she longed to pull him into her arms, longed to erase the anguish marring his handsome face.

"Linda finally begged me to take a break. It was the only time she ever actually demanded that I meet her for dinner. I didn't react to it very well. I said some pretty harsh things before I agreed to meet her at a restaurant near the hospital."

"I know that hospital. It's not in one of the better sections of D.C."

He gave a small, self-deprecating laugh. "I never even thought about that. If I had, Linda would still be alive."

"What happened?"

"We were supposed to meet there at nine. A gunshot came in at eight-thirty, ruptured aorta."

"That doesn't sound like the kind of injury you put on hold while you sip wine and decide between veal or fish."

"It isn't," he admitted. "But there were three other residents on that night."

Understanding dawned. "But you took it yourself and missed dinner."

"Apparently Linda got tired of waiting for me...again. She left the restaurant and walked toward the Metro. She caught a stray bullet when two punks were trying to settle a dispute over a pair of tennis shoes."

Destiny was quiet for several minutes, not really sure how to respond. "It wasn't your fault."

"Yes, it was," he told her. "She wouldn't have been in the wrong place at the wrong time if I'd had the common courtesy to show up."

"She could have called a cab," she suggested.

"She was my responsibility, Destiny. I should have been there for her. God knows she was there for me enough times. I couldn't even help her when they brought her in."

"You were there? In the ER?"

He got to his feet. "I was in the lounge, celebrating the fact that I'd just saved the life of a seventeen-year-old drug dealer."

"And you would have given anything if the drug dealer died, and you'd expended your talents on Linda."

He stood with his back to her and simply nodded.

"You were a surgeon, Wesley. Not a psychic. You had no way of knowing what would happen."

"But I knew then that I could no longer be a surgeon. I knew I'd never be able to put aside my anger and my bias. I had to give it up."

She went up behind him, slipping her arms around him, resting her cheek against his back. "I agree. But Wesley," she began in a slow, hesitant voice, "I'm not Linda. I don't expect you to protect me. And I'm not your responsibility."

He turned and cupped her face in his hands. His expression was one of deep, heartfelt agony. "Yes, you are."

"I'm a big girl," she told him with a small smile. "Whatever happens to me—"

"Don't you get it?" he asked softly. "I thought I could just lend a hand. I thought it would somehow make me feel redeemed for how terribly I neglected Linda.''

"And you have," she assured him. "You've been very kind and—''

"I love you, Destiny. I don't want to, but I do.''

"Do I say thank you, or slap you?'' she asked, holding her breath as she awaited his response.

Wesley sucked in a long, audible breath. "I didn't say that right.''

"Then you don't love me?''

His eyes burned into hers. "I *definitely* love you. I just didn't mean for it to happen.''

"So what are you telling me?''

"I'm not sure. All I know is that I couldn't stand to have history repeat itself.''

"I'm not Linda.''

Wesley held her against him, showering kisses on her hair. "I know that. I haven't even thought of Linda since the first time I kissed you. I was convinced I could never feel this way about a woman again. Until you.''

"Wesley?'' She stepped out of his embrace and met his eyes. "I couldn't take playing stand-in for a ghost.''

He smiled. "That's what I've been trying to explain. Being with you has exorcised all my ghosts. I feel alive again. And I want you in my life.''

Destiny hung her head. "You have lousy timing, Doctor. In case you've forgotten, I don't have much of a life these days.''

"I'm willing to work within those parameters.'' He gave her a small tug. "If you'll have me.'' He bent his head, his lips brushing the sensitive skin near her ear.

"Tell me how you feel, Destiny. Tell me I haven't been imagining things."

"You haven't."

"That romantic outburst did wonders for my ego."

"Sorry," she mumbled. "The truth is, I'm not completely sure of my feelings."

"What would it take for you to make up your mind?"

"I don't know that, either."

"Then I'll just have to try to persuade you."

Wesley carried her into the bedroom and made love to her in a whole new way. He was patient, careful and attentive to her every need. It was as if the man could read her mind, somehow know what she wanted even before she herself was sure.

Afterward, when she was safely curled in his arms, Destiny knew without question that she loved him. She also knew she couldn't offer him the happiness he sought. Tears spilled onto the pillowcase until she fell into an exhausted, dreamless sleep.

SHE AWAKENED TO THE AROMA of brewing coffee. Judging from the position of the sun in the sky, it was still early. Rubbing her tired, slightly swollen eyes with the back of her hand, she tossed aside the covers and started for the bathroom. The phone stopped her. Without thinking, she grabbed the receiver.

"Hello?"

"How's my girl?"

He sounds sober. "Fine, Dad. Where'd you run off to?"

"I'd like to take my little girl to breakfast. Can you meet me at the Customs House in about an hour?"

"What's the occasion?" she asked, instantly suspicious of her father's uncharacteristic invitation.

"Can't a father take his baby to breakfast?"

"Depends on who's paying," she quipped.

"Me," Carl answered. "I want to discuss something with you, so please don't bring your personal physician along."

Destiny felt herself frown. "What's up, Dad? You don't sound like yourself."

"Nothing's wrong," Carl answered after a brief hesitation. "Just do me this favor, please."

"Okay. I'll be there."

She was still slightly perplexed when she joined Wesley in the kitchen. She found him perched on one of the stools, headphones on his ears and his bare foot tapping in time to the silent melody.

She touched him on the shoulder, forcing him to look up from his open book. The huge smile he offered instantly erased her misgivings about her father's sudden desire for quality parenting time.

"Good morning," he purred as he spun and pulled her between his powerful thighs. He pushed off his headphones before kissing her hard on the mouth. "You taste good."

"I guess there is truth in advertising," she said. "The commercial guaranteed I'd have kissably fresh breath if I used their product."

"Definitely send them a testimonial. You didn't have to dress for breakfast," he added as he cast an admiring glance over her form-fitting purple dress.

"I have a breakfast date," she told him, watching as his expression grew predictably dark. "With my father."

Her explanation didn't exactly eradicate the misgivings clouding his eyes. Tugging off his glasses, Wesley said, "When did you speak to your father?"

"He called a little while ago. I guess you couldn't hear the phone with these on." She snapped the plastic cord of the headphones, which now hung limply around his neck like a stethoscope.

"Do you think this is a good idea? I should come with you."

"Calm down," she soothed, running her palms over the warm, bare flesh of his chest.

"I can't remain calm if you're going to do that."

Destiny took her hands out of his shirt and held them up in mock surrender. "I won't be gone long," she told him. "My father usually asks for cash in the first ten minutes."

His expression was one of concern. "I still don't think you should be wandering around alone."

"The guy's still in jail, right?"

"But there's still the matter of the woman."

Destiny stiffened slightly against the rigid muscle of his thighs. "We're meeting at the Customs House. That's a very public, very safe place."

"It will only take me a few—"

"Study," she told him as she got up on tiptoe and brushed a kiss against his mouth. "I'll be fine."

She stepped back and lifted the strap of her small purse over her head, angling it across her body. Her cheeks burned when she realized Wesley was staring rather intently at the outline of her breasts. "You're making this really difficult," she said in a hoarse voice.

"Not as difficult as you're making it for me to know you'll be out in public in that thing. It fits you like a second skin."

"It's supposed to," she said with a wink. "Which is why I only wear it when I'm meeting my father or some other paternalistic male. Speaking of which..." She paused and grabbed the pad next to the phone, then scribbled a number. "Would you mind calling Walter's office to find out how he got hold of those invoices? He's almost always there at ten. He's got a new secretary, but I haven't talked to her yet, so I don't know her name."

"Do you wear that dress when you have breakfast with Walter?" he mocked.

"Forget my dress." She sighed. "Will you do it?"

"Only if you promise to wear that for me sometime."

"Pervert."

"Tease," he called after her.

Destiny took a cab into the city, still wearing the giddy grin. She hadn't felt so good, so alive, since her early days back at David's club. Back when life was simple.

The Customs House was a rather imposing building, complete with dignified columns and an echoing foyer. Scanning the tall, narrow corridor, she frowned when she saw no sign of her father. Silently she wondered how many liquor stores her father had passed before he'd given in to his sickness.

Destiny marched over to the information booth and smiled at the uniformed woman behind the glass shield. "I'm looking for a man in his early fifties. About this tall? Gray ponytail."

"Sorry," she said. "Have you tried the straw market across the street? Lots of people wander over there when they're killing time."

"Thanks," Destiny said. "Is there a liquor store over there?"

"Yes. Down toward the end. Left side."

Taking her sunglasses from her head, Destiny slipped them on, a defense against the bright morning sun. Lack of sleep had left her pale eyes ultra light sensitive.

"C'mon, Dad," she mumbled as she walked to the corner to wait for the light.

She felt something hard and cold jab into her back before an ominous voice said, "I'm afraid your father's been delayed."

Chapter Eighteen

Wesley looked up from his book as the clock chimed for the tenth time. Grabbing the piece of paper Destiny had left behind, he moved to the phone, feeling strangely ill at ease. Of course, his state of mind was easy enough to explain. He'd bared his soul to her, only to discover that Destiny wasn't sure of her feelings. Then there was the matter of that dress. Every possessive cell of his body still regretted the fact that she had walked out of here looking like the most desirable, sexy woman alive.

"That's because she is," he mumbled as he dialed the phone.

"Law Officesss of Walter Sssomerfield."

His blood turned to ice when he heard the woman's pronounced speech impediment. Fear knotted his chest as the distinctive New Jersey dialect registered in his brain.

"Is Mr. Sommerfield in?" he asked, miraculously managing to keep his voice even.

"I'm sssorry, sssir," she answered. "Mr. Sssomerfield isss out of town. May I take a messsage?"

Wesley cursed and pressed the hang-up button. Rapidly he made the second call.

"Hello?"

"Shelby? Wesley. I need Dylan."

"Is something wrong?"

"Everything," he said. "I found out who is trying to kill Destiny."

"Hold on."

He filled Dylan in on the connection, then ran from the condo, silently praying he could find her before Sommerfield made his next move.

He left the Mercedes illegally parked on the street and jogged into the Customs House. When he saw no sign of Destiny or her father, Wesley went to the information desk.

"I'm looking for a blond woman. About five-two, one hundred pounds, wearing a purple dress?"

The woman eyed him curiously. "You don't look fifty, and you sure as hell don't got no ponytail."

"What?"

"She was here, all right. Looking for a gray-haired man with a ponytail."

"When was she here?"

"About half an hour ago. She went across the street to—"

Wesley didn't wait around for the rest of the woman's explanation. Adrenaline pumped through his veins as he reached his car and yanked the cellular phone from the console.

"Tanner."

"Dylan? They've got her."

"Slow down," his friend said. "Mackie is still in custody. I checked with the CPD—he's not scheduled for a bail hearing until eleven-thirty."

"It isn't the stalker," Wesley managed to say on a rush of breath. "I was right. Sommerfield has her."

"When? How?"

"I can't explain it all now, but I need help. I'm going to check the straw market, but I'll bet he's taken her someplace a little less public."

"I'll call CPD and be there in a flash. Wait for me by the east entrance."

Wesley tossed the phone back into the car and sprinted across to the crowded market. Thanks to his height, he could see nearly the full length of the narrow stalls. Ignoring the calls from the peddlers, he wove and pushed his way through the throng of people.

A sense of dread fell over him, coupled with a growing feeling of helplessness. Though he tried, he couldn't keep his mind from imagining Destiny in any number of torturous situations. He found himself teetering between rage and frenzied terror. Still he surged forward, desperate to find her.

He checked the shops and restaurants at the far end. Nothing. He searched the sidewalks on either side of the market. Then he saw something that tore the breath from his body.

Slowly, like a man walking to his own execution, Wesley moved over to the curb and reached down into the gutter. Gingerly he lifted the small purple purse and brushed off the grime from the street. He knew it was hers even before he opened it and checked the identification.

"No sign of her?" Dylan asked as he skidded to a halt at his side.

"Just this."

Dylan took the bag, his expression offering little hope. "I take it you're sure she had it when she left your place?"

"It matched her dress," he answered, his mind flashing back to his last vision of her. "Now what do we do?"

"I contacted the D.C. office and they're sending an agent over to interview the secretary with the speech impediment. I'm waiting for word—"

Dylan's portable phone began to ring and he pulled it from the pocket of his jacket. After a brief conversation, Wesley was relieved to see a faint flicker of optimism in his friend's eyes.

"C'mon," he said. "My car's just around the corner."

Dylan barked orders over the phone as he sped from the city. Wesley opened and closed his fists as he listened to Dylan broadcast the location where he believed Destiny was being held.

"How did you find that out?" he asked when Dylan tossed the phone onto the dash.

"The secretary was very accommodating."

"She was also the one blackmailing Gina. Any chance she was doing this on her own?"

Dylan shook his head. "She told the agents everything she knew."

"Including Sommerfield's reason for doing this. It doesn't make sense. Destiny said he treated her like a daughter."

"He blames her for his daughter's death."

"Why?"

Dylan caromed the car off a curb as he took a turn at high speed. "In his mind, Destiny convinced Samantha to try comedy. He apparently believes that Destiny is responsible for his daughter's drinking because she encouraged her in other ways."

"He'll kill her, won't he?" Wesley asked in a strangled voice.

"Not if I can help it."

SHE COULD ONLY communicate with her eyes. Walter had placed silver tape over her mouth and bound her hands and feet to the hard chair. She watched him through her tears, followed his erratic pacing in the small confines of the dingy motel room.

"You should have taken her keys that night," he was ranting. "She looked up to you."

Destiny wanted to tell him that she hadn't seen Sam that night. She'd been onstage in the hour preceding the girl's departure from the club. She struggled against the binding, feeling the tape rip the tiny hairs on her arm.

Wincing, she turned her head to check her father's condition. No change, but the blood no longer seemed to be dripping from the gash on his forehead. She turned angry eyes back to Walter, seeing him clearly, reading the insanity in his expression.

"How does it feel?" he rasped, moving close enough so that his hot breath stung her cheeks. "How do you like seeing someone you love dead?"

Destiny didn't react; she'd seen a small movement in her father's chest just minutes before. He was still alive, but not by much. She needed to get free if she had any hope of helping him.

She continued to stare at Walter, forcing herself not to react as she worked on the tape binding her wrists. Using her fingernail, she found the edge of the tape and began the painstaking task of peeling away the glue.

"I can't tell you how much I've hated you these past three years." Walter began to pace again, waving the small-caliber gun as he spoke. "I knew just killing you would be too easy. I wanted you on the brink of success. I wanted you right where Samantha was when you killed her. I made it happen. It was so easy. You jumped at the chance to go on the road. You jumped at the chance to write your own show. It was like taking a lamb to slaughter. Then when you garnered the attention of that demented man, Mackie, it was like a gift. Thanks to Gina, I knew I could easily torment you and leave Mackie holding the bag. Unfortunately now that the police know about him, I've had to alter my plan."

Walter stopped and took a drink from the bottle of water perched atop the scarred dresser. Destiny sucked in a deep breath, nearly choking on the stench of her own fear. One hard pull and she'd felt the tape give a little. All she needed was a bit more time.

"Time's up," Walter said with a sneer, his eyes narrow and filled with pure hatred. Reaching into the front pocket of his pants, he removed a silver cylinder and screwed it to the gun's muzzle. "The whole world knows your father is a violent drunk," he began. It will be a simple matter to have them believe that the two of you had an argument and he killed you in one of his drunken rages."

She began to thrash her head.

"You're thinking of the doctor," Walter said with an evil smile. "I'm going to arrange a little accident for him. That idiot I sent to the villa who stabbed Gina instead of you owes me one. Men like that have no conscience, but they do seem to possess an admirable sense of honor."

Walter took a step forward and cruelly laid the cold pistol in her lap while he put on his gloves. Methodically, and fully aware of the impact of his cruelty, he smiled at her as he prepared to shoot.

Lifting the gun, he took his monogrammed handkerchief and wiped it clean. He moved toward her father, and Destiny sprang into action.

Without hesitation she jerked her body and toppled the chair. They fell into a tangled mass. Destiny's head hit the floor with a thud that dulled her senses. She was only vaguely aware of the voices around her. All she could think about was covering her father with her own body. Lurching again, she felt the chair move at the same instant she heard the loud explosion from the gun. "Daddy!" she screamed against the tape.

"YOUR DAD'S OKAY," Wesley said for the fifth time in as many minutes. "The impact of the shot grazing his temple caused a concussion."

She stood cradled in the sanctuary of his arms. "He wanted me to watch my father die, then he was going to kill me."

"I know," he said as he rubbed her back.

"I can't believe there are two people on this earth who hate me so much."

"I love you."

"I love you, too, Wesley. I knew that all along. I was just afraid to admit it."

"I'm glad. But you're wrong about the number of people who hate you."

"There's more?" she asked, some of the lightness returning to her voice.

"Walter didn't make it. He died on the way in."

She was quiet for a long moment, content just to let him hold her. "He wasn't a bad man," she said finally.

"Depends on your perspective," Wesley said against her ear. "If Dylan hadn't pulled the trigger, I think I could have killed him with my bare hands."

"How's Dylan holding up?" she asked, tilting her head so that she could see his eyes.

"He did the only thing possible under the circumstances. He's a professional."

"Still," she reasoned, "I can't believe it won't affect him."

"It will affect all of us," Wesley told her as he wiped his thumb across her tearstained cheek. "I'll probably never get over the memory of bursting through that door and seeing Sommerfield standing over you with that gun up against your head.

She felt him shiver, so she tightened her hold. "I couldn't let him shoot my father."

"I understand. Just like Dylan couldn't let him shoot you." Wesley kissed her forehead softly and said, "Let's go home, Destiny. I need to be with you now. Besides, I hate police stations."

"Me, too," she agreed. "Just let me make a quick stop in the ladies' room, and we can be on our way. You go grab the car."

The sight of her own reflection was a vivid reminder of the events. Her wrists were raw and red from the tape, and her panty hose were practically shredded. She slipped into one of the stalls to remove them. She was only barely aware that another person had entered. Until she saw the tips of his shoes at her door.

"We aren't finished yet, Destiny. Not by a long shot."

Chapter Nineteen

Destiny finally found her voice and let out a loud scream. Wesley, trailed by Dylan and Shelby, rushed in.

"He was here, Mackie was here!" she said as she flew into Wesley's arms. "He ran out the back exit."

Dylan dashed out the exit while Wesley and Shelby administered comfort.

It took several minutes for Destiny to stop shaking. In fact, she wasn't totally calm until Wesley saw her safely back to the condo.

"How could that happen?" she asked as he pulled her across his lap.

"Apparently, he made bail."

"And that means he's free to continue tormenting me?"

"We'll go and see the prosecutor tomorrow. Maybe they can give us some options."

"I'm starting to think this will never be over," she said as she buried her face against his chest. "He got to me in the police station, for God's sake."

"We'll find a way to make it end," Wesley promised.

She saw such determination in his eyes that she very nearly believed it.

THOSE HOPES WERE DASHED the next day when she received the predictable word from the authorities. Unless—and until—Mackie did something more threatening than trespassing, there was nothing they could do. She couldn't even get a restraining order until she had actual proof of his harassment.

"This will make tonight a lot of fun," she mumbled as she slid into the passenger seat.

Wesley turned surprised eyes on her. "You aren't thinking of doing your show?"

"What else am I supposed to do?" she argued. "If I go into hiding, I'll never get what they need for a judge to order him to stay away from me."

"And what do you think that will accomplish?" Wesley asked. It was the first time he'd directed his anger at her.

"He'll have to stay at least two hundred yards away from me."

"No, Destiny," Wesley said with patient annoyance. "It means you'll have a piece of paper that he probably won't respect any more than he respects the law."

She felt her own temper flare. "What do you suggest? That I do what Dylan says and start all over again in some strange town where I can't contact my family or perform?"

"Yeah," he grated, "but you'd be alive."

She let out a disgusted breath and stared straight ahead.

"I'll come with you."

"What?" She turned and took in his earnest expression

"I'll come with you. I'll change my name and become a quiet country doctor."

She regarded him cautiously. "You're joking, right? You really think I could live with myself if I took you away from your family, not to mention your practice?"

Wesley raised his hands. "Do you see any practice here? I'm perfectly free to go with you and establish a nice, quiet life together."

"Where you can be a doctor," she said. "And what can I be? A doctor's wife and nothing else? I'm a performer, Wesley. Do you really think I could be satisfied tucked away in some anonymous community doing nothing but waiting for you to come home for dinner?"

Anger flashed in his eyes. "I'd rather see you at dinner than visit your grave."

"How bad was the fight?" Rose inquired the moment Destiny opened the door.

"Do you have radar?" Destiny asked. "Or did he come crying to you?"

"Hold on," Rose said, her expression cautionary. "My son *never* comes crying to me about anything. I just happened to be in the office when he commandeered Shelby."

"What for?"

"I don't have a clue, but he and Dylan definitely had something in mind. I figured they were on their way over here."

Destiny stepped aside and waved her arm. "I'm all by my lonesome, as you can see. And I've got to get ready to go to work."

Ignoring her comment, Rose sashayed into the living room and arranged herself on the sofa. "You don't have to get ready—you don't have a job."

Destiny's mouth fell open.

Rose simply offered a Cheshire-cat smile. "Shelby and I decided to pay off the cancellation clause of our contract. Show's closed."

"That isn't fair!" she cried.

Rose's green eyes narrowed. "Mackie already stabbed Gina to get to you. We had a meeting, and none of us are willing to risk the lives of our patrons so that you can prove you're smarter than a deranged lunatic."

Destiny's mouth snapped shut.

Blowing on her nails, Rose buffed them on the collar of her zebra-print blouse. "We've taken care of Gina."

"What do you mean?"

"The police found her in a small motel near Bohicket."

"Is she all right?"

"Just dandy, and she's got a new job."

Destiny fell into the chair, utterly shocked. "Doing what? She's still recuperating."

"Nothing too strenuous. She's helping Shelby with the kids."

"Children aren't strenuous?" Destiny challenged.

"Why don't you and Wesley have a couple? See for yourself."

"This isn't about me and Wesley," she said with a groan. "Gina doesn't know anything about kids."

"She'll catch on," Rose said. "They're starting her out slowly. She's only covering nap time."

"Why are you doing this?" Destiny asked.

There was a flash of sadness in Rose's green eyes. "Because I always do what's best for my sons. Even if it means letting them go."

The words hit her like an arrow piercing her heart. "Wesley's leaving?" she asked.

"As soon as possible," Rose stated firmly. "And you—"

Rose was cut off by the arrival of Dylan, Wesley, Shelby and a woman with long blond hair brushed forward to hide her features.

Wesley came over and placed an unexpected kiss on her slightly parted lips. "Destiny Talbott, meet Jennifer Sanders."

"Hello," Destiny stammered.

The woman raised her head. The action caused several strands of her blond hair to fall back on her shoulders, revealing a long, jagged scar that ran from the corner of her eye down the side of her face. It disappeared beneath the high collar of her shirt.

"Miss Talbott," she acknowledged politely.

Destiny was struck by more than just the scar. There was a strong resemblance between herself and the small-framed woman standing in the center of the room.

Shelby went and took Jennifer's hand, guiding her to a seat. Then she looked at Destiny and said, "Jennifer has a few things to tell you."

After an encouraging hug from Shelby, the woman began to speak in a small, quavering voice. "I met Ronald Mackie ten years ago. We worked together at an engineering firm in Washington."

"My Ronald Mackie?" Destiny asked.

She nodded. "We went out a few times, but we didn't have much in common. I'm the serious type. Opera and foreign films. He's country music and Abbott and Costello. He even took me to the club in Baltimore to see you."

Destiny shook. That man had been watching her for more than a decade.

"Anyway, after I told him I didn't want to see him, he started following me, sending me long letters. I took them to the police and got a restraining order."

"Good for you," Destiny said, unable to think of anything more appropriate.

Jennifer let out a small, mirthless laugh. "That's where you're wrong," she admitted sadly. "He violated the restraining order by leaving dolls on my doorstep."

"I've gotten a few of those."

"I had him arrested."

"Then what's he doing out now?"

Jennifer met her eyes. "It's the system, Miss Talbott. We have to help ourselves."

"What did you do?"

"I stood up to him," Jennifer said calmly. "I was determined that I wasn't going to let him destroy my life." Jennifer gathered her hair in a ponytail. "I had him arrested again. He served three months and then he was released. That's when he did this." She ran her finger along the path of the ugly scar.

"And that wasn't enough to put him behind bars?"

"For another eighteen months."

"Then what did he do?" Destiny asked.

Jennifer lowered her eyes. "I didn't stick around to find out. I changed my name and started a new life someplace safe."

"Then how did you find out about me?" Destiny asked.

"He found me," she answered, pointing to Dylan. "And she convinced me to come out of hiding long enough to convince you to do the same thing I did."

Shelby hugged the woman again.

"But what about your family? What about—"

"The alternative was worse," Jennifer interrupted quietly. "Mackie didn't just cut my face, Miss Talbott. I have thirty-seven different scars on my body as a result of being held captive by that man for four horrifying days."

"USING JENNIFER SANDERS was a cheap tactic," she told Wesley when they were alone.

"Dylan's idea," Wesley countered as he flicked open the top button of her blouse. "But I agreed wholeheartedly."

"It was a terrible ploy to scare me into doing what you want."

He nuzzled her neck. "Into doing what was right."

"I have a hard time concentrating when you do that."

"Good," he murmured against her throat. "You're not supposed to concentrate when I'm seducing you."

"You don't have to do this," she said halfheartedly. "I've already agreed to let Dylan arrange to relocate me."

"Us," Wesley corrected as his hand slipped inside and found her breast.

Destiny sucked in an excited breath. "I can't let you do that, Wesley. I can't force you to abandon your family and—"

"Don't," he interrupted, lifting his head and meeting her eyes. "I love you, Destiny. I want to be with you. Whether it's in the wilds of Alaska or in a hut on Bora-Bora. We can both contact our families through Dylan, and he'll make sure we know when and if Mackie is no longer a threat. Until then, you promised to marry me and I'm holding you to it."

"Wesley?" she began as she unbuttoned the waistband of his jeans.

"Yes?"

"If it's the wilds of Alaska, the deal's off."

"I think..." he began, when a scraping sound caught their attention. Wesley placed a finger to his lips and moved soundlessly over to the French doors. "Holy—"

Reacting to the surprise in his voice, Destiny raced to him. Through large, horrified eyes she saw first one, then a second gloved hand hook over the railing.

"Call the cops!" Wesley shouted. "Try Dylan's car phone, too."

Destiny wasted no time making the calls. By the time she returned to the balcony, all hell had broken loose. Wesley and Ronald Mackie were wrestling near the edge of the wooden railing. She felt utterly helpless as she watched them career from the wall to the railing, over and over again.

She called out, trying to warn Wesley that the bolts holding the railing were beginning to pull free of the wall. Her mind flashed horrid images of the railing giving way, and the man she loved falling seven stories to a grisly death.

Her eyes scanned the balcony, desperate for some sort of weapon. Then she remembered. Twirling on the ball of her foot, she went into the living room and found her weapon. Clutching it tightly as she heard a painful grunt escape through Wesley's pained grimace, she lunged forward and jabbed Mackie in the ribs with the marble banana.

The force of the blow sent him reeling backward. He hit the weakened railing, and time slowed as she heard the sound of the wood splintering just before it gave way.

Mackie, his face a grotesque contortion with the knowledge of what was happening, grabbed at Wesley as he began to fall.

"Hold my arm!" Wesley said.

The gloved hand gripped his wrist. The man's weight immediately sent Wesley sprawling so that he was lying on the cement, with Mackie dangling over the edge.

Destiny moved forward and met the eyes of her tormentor. He looked up at her, pleading.

"Let him fall," she said quietly, remembering Gina, the dolls and the ragged scar on Jennifer's face.

"I can't," Wesley said, breathing hard between words. "I took an oath to save lives . . . even his."

Wesley strained to make progress, but the smooth leather of Mackie's glove didn't provide enough traction. "Get behind me," he yelled. "Keep me stable while I try to get him back on the balcony."

Destiny moved, knowing in her heart that she was doing the right thing, but her emotions still struggled with the idea of assisting a man who was so evil. She had reached Wesley's knees when she heard the unmistakable sound of a gunshot.

Her throat closed in fear as she turned, expecting to find Wesley mortally wounded.

His head was down, his arms limp in front of his head. Instinctively, she threw herself on him, crying his name.

"It wasn't me," she heard him say.

Crawling over him, Destiny looked at the scene below. "Oh, heavens," she muttered before scrambling off him.

The figure of the small blond woman standing over the crumpled form was unmistakable. "That's Jennifer. What on earth . . ."

"I have a feeling," Wesley began as he pulled himself into a sitting position, "that Jennifer just found a way to protect herself."

"WHAT WILL THEY DO TO HER?" Destiny asked Dylan.

"Probation's my guess."

It was a somber group assembled at The Rose Tattoo. Everyone, Destiny included, was still adjusting. She was also trying to adjust to Wesley's odd behavior. Ever since the ambulance had removed Mackie's body, Wesley had been quiet, pensive.

Even though she was now free of danger and able to keep her own identity, it seemed as if she was about to lose the most important part of her life—Wesley. There was no need for him to give up his life for her, no threat of danger. He could stay in Charleston and shrink every head in town.

"Why the frown?" he asked.

She met his gaze. "Could we go out on the porch and talk?"

He took her hand, and she realized it was the first time he'd touched her since the afternoon. She clung to him, sensing impending doom.

The early-evening air was cool, almost chilly. Like her companion.

Wesley held out one of the high-backed chairs for her and then sat across from her. Destiny tried not to read too much into the action. So what if he hadn't opted for the cozy, romantic swing?

"You wanted to talk to me?"

Another bad sign, she decided. That flat, analytic tone made her suck in a fortifying breath. "I guess David told you that the network is still interested in the show?"

"Uh-huh."

"They want me to come to California, after all."

"Uh-huh."

"They think all the press I'll get over this Mackie thing might even turn out to be a positive."

"Uh-huh."

"Wesley," she groaned, grabbing his hand. "I'm baring my soul here and you've suddenly developed a vocabulary that wouldn't give Chad a run for his money."

Raking his hand through his hair, Wesley removed his glasses and placed them gently on the table.

"I'm just waiting for you to ask the right question."

Perplexed, Destiny frowned. "What question?"

"I told you once that I'd be willing to give up everything to be with you. At the time I made that offer, you didn't have any choice. You had to go into hiding, or Mackie might have killed you."

"I know that."

"Things have changed."

She looked deeply into his eyes. "Things? Or your feelings for me?"

"Things," he answered quietly. "You don't need me now, Destiny. It looks like things in L.A. will work out without Walter Sommerfield. You'll be able to do the thing you love most—perform."

"You're wrong," she told him as she got up and went over to sit on his lap. "I love you most, Wesley. L.A., the show, none of it will mean anything if you aren't there to share it with me."

She saw the beginnings of a smile tug at the corners of his mouth. "So does this mean you're going to ask me?"

"Ask you what?"

"Ask me to be the husband of an actress and nothing else?"

"Ouch," she said. "I guess I did disparage the idea of being your wife, didn't I?"

"A little."

"Will you come with me, Wesley? You can still practice in L.A.," she pleaded. "Hell, in L.A. you'll probably have a waiting list ten minutes after you hang out your shingle.''

His expression grew serious. "Are you sure this is what you want?"

"Of course. We're talking L.A. here, not the wilds of Alaska."

He kissed her with enough tenderness to last a lifetime.

Take 4 bestselling love stories FREE

Plus get a FREE surprise gift!

Special Limited-time Offer

Mail to Harlequin Reader Service®

3010 Walden Avenue
P.O. Box 1867
Buffalo, N.Y. 14269-1867

YES! Please send me 4 free Harlequin Intrigue® novels and my free surprise gift. Then send me 4 brand-new novels every month. Bill me at the low price of $2.44 each plus 25¢ delivery and applicable sales tax, if any.* That's the complete price and a savings of over 10% off the cover prices—quite a bargain! I understand that accepting the books and gift places me under no obligation ever to buy any books. I can always return a shipment and cancel at any time. Even if I never buy another book from Harlequin, the 4 free books and the surprise gift are mine to keep forever.

181 BPA ANRK

Name	(PLEASE PRINT)	
Address		Apt. No.
City	State	Zip

This offer is limited to one order per household and not valid to present Harlequin Intrigue® subscribers. *Terms and prices are subject to change without notice.
Sales tax applicable in N.Y.

UINT-295 ©1990 Harlequin Enterprises Limited

HARLEQUIN®

Don't miss these Harlequin favorites by some of our most distinguished authors!
And now, you can receive a discount by ordering two or more titles!

HT #25559	JUST ANOTHER PRETTY FACE by Candace Schuler	$2.99	☐
HT #25616	THE BOUNTY HUNTER by Vicki Lewis Thompson	$2.99 U.S./$3.50 CAN.	☐
HP #11667	THE SPANISH CONNECTION by Kay Thorpe	$2.99 U.S./$3.50 CAN.	☐
HP #11701	PRACTISE TO DECEIVE by Sally Wentworth	$2.99 U.S./$3.50 CAN.	☐
HR #03268	THE BAD PENNY by Susan Fox	$2.99	☐
HR #03340	THE NUTCRACKER PRINCE by Rebecca Winters	$2.99 U.S./$3.50 CAN.	☐
HS #70540	FOR THE LOVE OF IVY by Barbara Kaye	$3.39	☐
HS #70596	DANCING IN THE DARK by Lynn Erickson	$3.50	☐
HI #22196	CHILD'S PLAY by Bethany Campbell	$2.89	☐
HI #22304	BEARING GIFTS by Aimée Thurlo	$2.99 U.S./$3.50 CAN.	☐
HAR #16538	KISSED BY THE SEA by Rebecca Flanders	$3.50 U.S./$3.99 CAN.	☐
HAR #16553	THE MARRYING TYPE by Judith Arnold	$3.50 U.S./$3.99 CAN.	☐
HH #28847	DESIRE MY LOVE by Miranda Jarrett	$3.99 U.S./$4.50 CAN	☐
HH #28848	VOWS by Margaret Moore	$3.99 U.S./$4.50 CAN.	☐

(limited quantities available on certain titles)

	AMOUNT	$
DEDUCT:	**10% DISCOUNT FOR 2+ BOOKS**	$
	POSTAGE & HANDLING ($1.00 for one book, 50¢ for each additional)	$
	APPLICABLE TAXES*	$_____
	TOTAL PAYABLE	$_____
	(check or money order—please do not send cash)	

To order, complete this form and send it, along with a check or money order for the
total above, payable to Harlequin Books, to: **In the U.S.:** 3010 Walden Avenue,
P.O. Box 9047, Buffalo, NY 14269-9047; **In Canada:** P.O. Box 613, Fort Erie, Ontario,
L2A 5X3.

Name: _____

Address: _____ City: _____

State/Prov.: _____ Zip/Postal Code: _____

*New York residents remit applicable sales taxes.
Canadian residents remit applicable GST and provincial taxes.

HBACK-JS2

RUGGED. SEXY. HEROIC.

OUTLAWS and HEROES

Stony Carlton—A lone wolf determined never to be tied down.

Gabriel Taylor—Accused and found guilty by small-town gossip.

Clay Barker—At Revenge Unlimited, he *is* the law.

JOAN JOHNSTON, DALLAS SCHULZE and MALLORY RUSH, three of romance fiction's biggest names, have created three unforgettable men—modern heroes who have the courage to fight for what is right....

OUTLAWS AND HEROES—available in September wherever Harlequin books are sold.

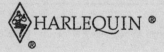

HARLEQUIN ®

As a *Privileged Woman,*
you'll be entitled to all these *Free Benefits.*
And *Free Gifts,* too.

To thank you for buying our books, we've designed an exclusive FREE program called *PAGES & PRIVILEGES™*. You can enroll with just one Proof of Purchase, and get the kind of luxuries that, until now, you could only read about.

*B*IG HOTEL DISCOUNTS

A privileged woman stays in the finest hotels. And so can you—at up to 60% off! Imagine standing in a hotel check-in line and watching as the guest in front of you pays $150 for the same room that's only costing you $60. Your *Pages & Privileges* discounts are good at Sheraton, Marriott, Best Western, Hyatt and thousands of other fine hotels all over the U.S., Canada and Europe.

*F*REE DISCOUNT TRAVEL SERVICE

A privileged woman is always jetting to romantic places. When you fly, just make one phone call for the lowest published airfare at time of booking—or double the difference back! PLUS—

you'll get a $25 voucher to use the first time you book a flight AND 5% cash back on every ticket you buy thereafter through the travel service!

HI-PP4A

FREE GIFTS!

A privileged woman is always getting wonderful gifts.
Luxuriate in rich fragrances that will stir your senses (and his). This gift-boxed assortment of fine perfumes includes three popular scents, each in a beautiful designer bottle. <u>Truly Lace</u>...This luxurious fragrance unveils your sensuous side. <u>L'Effleur</u>...discover the romance of the Victorian era with this soft floral. <u>Muguet des bois</u>...a single note floral of singular beauty.

YOURS FREE!

$50 VALUE

FREE INSIDER TIPS LETTER

A privileged woman is always informed. And you'll be, too, with our free letter full of fascinating information and sneak previews of upcoming books.

MORE GREAT GIFTS & BENEFITS TO COME

A privileged woman always has a lot to look forward to. And so will you. You get all these wonderful FREE gifts and benefits now with only one purchase...and there are no additional purchases required. However, each additional retail purchase of Harlequin and Silhouette books brings you a step closer to even more great FREE benefits like half-price movie tickets... and even more FREE gifts.

L'Effleur...This basketful of romance lets you discover L'Effleur from head to toe, heart to home.

Truly Lace...
A basket spun with the sensuous luxuries of Truly Lace, including Dusting Powder in a reusable satin and lace covered box.

Complete the Enrollment Form in the front of this book and mail it with this Proof of Purchase.

PROOF OF PURCHASE
Offer expires October 31, 1996

HL-PP4